'Emotionally shattering . . . *The Road* affirms belief in the tender pricelessness of the here and now. In creating an exquisite nightmare, it does not add to the cruelty and ugliness of our times; it warns us now how much we have to lose . . . Beauty and goodness are here aplenty and we should think about them. While we can'

Alan Warner, *Guardian*

'Nameless they remain, b̶u̶t̶   ie, some deep sy   able to us, causes u   heir fates, and so   f what m

Cli

'Cormac McCarthy's new   not of an individual but of all hum   y, feels very real. Part of the achievement of *The Road* is its poetic description of landscapes from which the possibility of poetry would seem to have been stripped, along with their ability to support life'

Adam Mars-Jones, *Observer*

The Road

CORMAC MCCARTHY is the author of ten acclaimed novels, most recently *The Road*. Among his honours are the Pulitzer Prize for Fiction and the PEN/Saul Bellow Award for lifetime achievement in American literature.

CORMAC McCARTHY

The Road

PICADOR

First published 2006 as a Borzoi Book by Alfred A. Knopf,
a division of Random House, Inc., New York
and simultaneously in Canada by Random House of Canada Limited, Toronto

First published in Great Britain 2006 by Picador

First published in paperback 2007 by Picador

This edition first published 2010 by Picador
an imprint of Pan Macmillan, a division of Macmillan Publishers Limited
Pan Macmillan, 20 New Wharf Road, London N1 9RR
Basingstoke and Oxford
Associated companies throughout the world
www.panmacmillan.com

ISBN 978-0-330-51300-5

7 9 8 6

A CIP catalogue record for this book is available from
the British Library.

Printed in the UK by CPI Mackays, Chatham ME5 8TD

This book is dedicated to

JOHN FRANCIS MCCARTHY

When he woke in the woods in the dark and the cold of the night he'd reach out to touch the child sleeping beside him. Nights dark beyond darkness and the days more gray each one than what had gone before. Like the onset of some cold glaucoma dimming away the world. His hand rose and fell softly with each precious breath. He pushed away the plastic tarpaulin and raised himself in the stinking robes and blankets and looked toward the east for any light but there was none. In the dream from which he'd wakened he had wandered in a cave where the child led him by the hand. Their light playing over the wet flowstone walls. Like pilgrims in a fable swallowed up and lost among the inward parts of some granitic beast. Deep stone flues where the water dripped and sang. Tolling in the silence the minutes of the earth and the hours and the days of it and the years without cease. Until they stood in a great stone room where lay a black and ancient lake. And on the far shore a creature that raised its dripping mouth from the rimstone pool and stared into the light with eyes dead white and sightless as the eggs of spiders. It swung its head low over the water as if to take the scent of what it could not see. Crouching there pale and naked and translucent, its alabaster bones cast up in shadow on the rocks behind it. Its bowels, its beating heart. The brain that pulsed in a dull glass bell. It swung its head from side to side and then gave out a low moan and turned and lurched away and loped soundlessly into the dark.

With the first gray light he rose and left the boy sleeping and walked out to the road and squatted and studied the country to the south. Barren, silent, godless. He thought the month was October but he wasnt sure. He hadnt kept a calendar for years. They were moving south. There'd be no surviving another winter here.

When it was light enough to use the binoculars he glassed the valley below. Everything paling away into the murk. The soft ash blowing in loose swirls over the blacktop. He studied what he could see. The segments of road down there among the dead trees. Looking for anything of color. Any movement. Any trace of standing smoke. He lowered the glasses and pulled down the cotton mask from his face and wiped his nose on the back of his wrist and then glassed the country again. Then he just sat there holding the binoculars and watching the ashen daylight congeal over the land. He knew only that the child was his warrant. He said: If he is not the word of God God never spoke.

When he got back the boy was still asleep. He pulled the blue plastic tarp off of him and folded it and carried it out to the grocery cart and packed it and came back with their plates and some cornmeal cakes in a plastic bag and a plastic bottle of syrup. He spread the small tarp they used for a table on the ground and laid everything out and he took the pistol from his belt and laid it on the cloth and then he just sat watching the boy sleep. He'd pulled away his mask in the night and it was buried somewhere in the blankets. He watched the boy and he looked out through the trees toward the road. This was not a safe place. They could be seen from the road now it was day. The boy turned in the blankets. Then he opened his eyes. Hi, Papa, he said.

I'm right here.

I know.

An hour later they were on the road. He pushed the cart and both he and the boy carried knapsacks. In the knapsacks were essential things. In case they had to abandon the cart and make a run for it. Clamped to the handle of the cart was a chrome motorcycle mirror that he used to watch the road behind them. He shifted the pack higher on his shoulders and looked out over the wasted country. The road was empty. Below in the little valley the still gray serpentine of a river. Motionless and precise. Along the shore a burden of dead reeds. Are you okay? he said. The boy nodded. Then they set out along the blacktop in the gunmetal light, shuffling through the ash, each the other's world entire.

They crossed the river by an old concrete bridge and a few miles on they came upon a roadside gas station. They stood in the road and studied it. I think we should check it out, the man said. Take a look. The weeds they forded fell to dust about them. They crossed the broken asphalt apron and found the tank for the pumps. The cap was gone and the man dropped to his elbows to smell the pipe but the odor of gas was only a rumor, faint and stale. He stood and looked over the building. The pumps standing with their hoses oddly still in place. The windows intact. The door to the service bay was open and he went in. A standing metal toolbox against one wall. He went through the drawers but there was nothing there that he could use. Good half-inch drive sockets. A ratchet. He stood looking around the garage. A metal barrel full of trash. He went into the office. Dust and ash everywhere. The boy stood in the door. A metal desk, a cashregister. Some old automotive manuals, swollen and sodden. The linoleum was stained and curling from the leaking roof. He crossed to the desk and stood there. Then he picked up the phone and dialed the number of his father's house in that long ago. The boy watched him. What are you doing? he said.

A quarter mile down the road he stopped and looked back. We're not thinking, he said. We have to go back. He pushed the cart off the road and tilted it over where it could not be seen and they left their packs and went back to the station. In the service bay he dragged out the steel

5

trashdrum and tipped it over and pawed out all the quart plastic oilbottles. Then they sat in the floor decanting them of their dregs one by one, leaving the bottles to stand upside down draining into a pan until at the end they had almost a half quart of motor oil. He screwed down the plastic cap and wiped the bottle off with a rag and hefted it in his hand. Oil for their little slutlamp to light the long gray dusks, the long gray dawns. You can read me a story, the boy said. Cant you, Papa? Yes, he said. I can.

On the far side of the river valley the road passed through a stark black burn. Charred and limbless trunks of trees stretching away on every side. Ash moving over the road and the sagging hands of blind wire strung from the blackened lightpoles whining thinly in the wind. A burned house in a clearing and beyond that a reach of meadow-lands stark and gray and a raw red mudbank where a roadworks lay abandoned. Farther along were billboards advertising motels. Everything as it once had been save faded and weathered. At the top of the hill they stood in the cold and the wind, getting their breath. He looked at the boy. I'm all right, the boy said. The man put his hand on his shoulder and nodded toward the open country below them. He got the binoculars out of the cart and stood in the road and glassed the plain down there where the shape of a city stood in the grayness like a charcoal drawing sketched across the waste. Nothing to see. No smoke. Can I see? the boy said. Yes. Of course you can. The boy leaned on the cart and adjusted the wheel. What do you see? the man said. Nothing. He lowered the glasses. It's raining. Yes, the man said. I know.

They left the cart in a gully covered with the tarp and made their way up the slope through the dark poles of the standing trees to where he'd seen a running ledge of rock and they sat under the rock overhang and watched the gray sheets of rain blow across the valley. It was very cold. They sat huddled together wrapped each in a blanket over their coats and after a while the rain stopped and there was just the dripping in the woods.

When it had cleared they went down to the cart and pulled away the tarp and got their blankets and the things they would need for the night. They went back up the hill and made their camp in the dry dirt under the rocks and the man sat with his arms around the boy trying to warm him. Wrapped in the blankets, watching the nameless dark come to enshroud them. The gray shape of the city vanished in the night's onset like an apparition and he lit the little lamp and set it back out of the wind. Then they walked out to the road and he took the boy's hand and they went to the top of the hill where the road crested and where they could see out over the darkening country to the south, standing there in the wind, wrapped in their blankets, watching for any sign of a fire or a lamp. There was nothing. The lamp in the rocks on the side of the hill was little more than a mote of light and after a while they walked back. Everything too wet to make a fire. They ate their poor meal cold and lay down in their bedding with the lamp between them. He'd brought the boy's book but the boy was too tired for reading. Can we leave the lamp on till I'm asleep? he said. Yes. Of course we can.

He was a long time going to sleep. After a while he turned and looked at the man. His face in the small light streaked with black from the rain like some old world thespian. Can I ask you something? he said.

Yes. Of course.

Are we going to die?

Sometime. Not now.

And we're still going south.

Yes.

So we'll be warm.

Yes.

Okay.

Okay what?

Nothing. Just okay.

Go to sleep.

Okay.

I'm going to blow out the lamp. Is that okay?

Yes. That's okay.

And then later in the darkness: Can I ask you some-thing?

Yes. Of course you can.

What would you do if I died?

If you died I would want to die too.

So you could be with me?

Yes. So I could be with you.

Okay.

. . .

He lay listening to the water drip in the woods. Bedrock, this. The cold and the silence. The ashes of the late world carried on the bleak and temporal winds to and fro in the void. Carried forth and scattered and carried forth again. Everything uncoupled from its shoring. Unsupported in the ashen air. Sustained by a breath, trembling and brief. If only my heart were stone.

He woke before dawn and watched the gray day break. Slow and half opaque. He rose while the boy slept and pulled on his shoes and wrapped in his blanket he walked out through the trees. He descended into a gryke in the stone and there he crouched coughing and he coughed for a long time. Then he just knelt in the ashes. He raised his face to the paling day. Are you there? he whispered. Will I see you at the last? Have you a neck by which to throttle you? Have you a heart? Damn you eternally have you a soul? Oh God, he whispered. Oh God.

They passed through the city at noon of the day following. He kept the pistol to hand on the folded tarp on top of the cart. He kept the boy close to his side. The city was mostly burned. No sign of life. Cars in the street caked with ash, everything covered with ash and dust. Fossil tracks in the dried sludge. A corpse in a doorway dried to leather. Grimacing at the day. He pulled the boy closer. Just remember that the things you put into your head are there forever, he said. You might want to think about that.

You forget some things, dont you?

Yes. You forget what you want to remember and you remember what you want to forget.

There was a lake a mile from his uncle's farm where he and his uncle used to go in the fall for firewood. He sat in the back of the rowboat trailing his hand in the cold wake while his uncle bent to the oars. The old man's feet in their black kid shoes braced against the uprights. His straw hat. His cob pipe in his teeth and a thin drool swinging from the pipebowl. He turned to take a sight on the far shore, cradling the oarhandles, taking the pipe from his mouth to wipe his chin with the back of his hand. The shore was lined with birchtrees that stood bone pale against the dark of the evergreens beyond. The edge of the lake a riprap of twisted stumps, gray and weathered, the windfall trees of a hurricane years past. The trees themselves had long been sawed for firewood and carried away. His uncle turned the boat and shipped the oars and they drifted over the sandy shallows until the transom grated in the sand. A dead perch lolling belly up in the clear water. Yellow leaves. They left their shoes on the warm painted boards and dragged the boat up onto the beach and set out the anchor at the end of its rope. A lardcan poured with concrete with an eyebolt in the center. They walked along the shore while his uncle studied the treestumps, puffing at his pipe, a manila rope coiled over his shoulder. He picked one out and they turned it over, using the roots for leverage, until they got it half floating in the water. Trousers rolled to the knee but still they got wet. They tied the rope to a cleat at the rear of the boat and rowed back across the lake, jerking the stump slowly behind them. By then it was already evening. Just the slow periodic rack and shuffle of the oarlocks. The lake dark glass and windowlights coming on along the shore. A radio somewhere. Neither of them had spoken a word. This was the perfect day of his childhood. This the day to shape the days upon.

They bore on south in the days and weeks to follow. Solitary and dogged. A raw hill country. Aluminum houses.

At times they could see stretches of the interstate highway below them through the bare stands of secondgrowth timber. Cold and growing colder. Just beyond the high gap in the mountains they stood and looked out over the great gulf to the south where the country as far as they could see was burned away, the blackened shapes of rock standing out of the shoals of ash and billows of ash rising up and blowing downcountry through the waste. The track of the dull sun moving unseen beyond the murk.

They were days fording that cauterized terrain. The boy had found some crayons and painted his facemask with fangs and he trudged on uncomplaining. One of the front wheels of the cart had gone wonky. What to do about it? Nothing. Where all was burnt to ash before them no fires were to be had and the nights were long and dark and cold beyond anything they'd yet encountered. Cold to crack the stones. To take your life. He held the boy shivering against him and counted each frail breath in the blackness.

He woke to the sound of distant thunder and sat up. The faint light all about, quivering and sourceless, refracted in the rain of drifting soot. He pulled the tarp about them and he lay awake a long time listening. If they got wet there'd be no fires to dry by. If they got wet they would probably die.

The blackness he woke to on those nights was sightless and impenetrable. A blackness to hurt your ears with listening. Often he had to get up. No sound but the wind in the bare and blackened trees. He rose and stood tottering in that cold autistic dark with his arms outheld for balance while the vestibular calculations in his skull cranked out their reckonings. An old chronicle. To seek out the upright. No fall but preceded by a declination. He took great marching steps into the nothingness, counting them against his return. Eyes closed, arms oaring. Upright to what? Something nameless in the night, lode or matrix. To which he and the stars were common satellite. Like the great pendulum in its rotunda scribing through the long day movements of the universe of which you may say it knows nothing and yet know it must.

It took two days to cross that ashen scabland. The road beyond ran along the crest of a ridge where the barren woodland fell away on every side. It's snowing, the boy said. He looked at the sky. A single gray flake sifting down. He caught it in his hand and watched it expire there like the last host of christendom.

They pushed on together with the tarp pulled over them. The wet gray flakes twisting and falling out of nothing. Gray slush by the roadside. Black water running from under the sodden drifts of ash. No more balefires on the distant ridges. He thought the bloodcults must have all consumed one another. No one traveled this road. No roadagents, no marauders. After a while they came to a roadside garage and they stood within the open door and looked out at the gray sleet gusting down out of the high country.

They collected some old boxes and built a fire in the floor and he found some tools and emptied out the cart and sat working on the wheel. He pulled the bolt and bored out the collet with a hand drill and resleeved it with a section of pipe he'd cut to length with a hacksaw. Then he bolted it all back together and stood the cart upright and wheeled it around the floor. It ran fairly true. The boy sat watching everything.

In the morning they went on. Desolate country. A boarhide nailed to a barndoor. Ratty. Wisp of a tail. Inside the barn three bodies hanging from the rafters, dried and dusty among the wan slats of light. There could be something here, the boy said. There could be some corn or something. Let's go, the man said.

Mostly he worried about their shoes. That and food. Always food. In an old batboard smokehouse they found a ham gambreled up in a high corner. It looked like something fetched from a tomb, so dried and drawn. He cut into it with his knife. Deep red and salty meat inside. Rich and good. They fried it that night over their fire, thick slices of it, and put the slices to simmer with a tin of beans. Later he woke in the dark and he thought that he'd heard bulldrums beating somewhere in the low dark hills. Then the wind shifted and there was just the silence.

. . .

In dreams his pale bride came to him out of a green and leafy canopy. Her nipples pipeclayed and her rib bones painted white. She wore a dress of gauze and her dark hair was carried up in combs of ivory, combs of shell. Her smile, her downturned eyes. In the morning it was snowing again. Beads of small gray ice strung along the lightwires overhead.

He mistrusted all of that. He said the right dreams for a man in peril were dreams of peril and all else was the call of languor and of death. He slept little and he slept poorly. He dreamt of walking in a flowering wood where birds flew before them he and the child and the sky was aching blue but he was learning how to wake himself from just such siren worlds. Lying there in the dark with the uncanny taste of a peach from some phantom orchard fading in his mouth. He thought if he lived long enough the world at last would all be lost. Like the dying world the newly blind inhabit, all of it slowly fading from memory.

From daydreams on the road there was no waking. He plodded on. He could remember everything of her save her scent. Seated in a theatre with her beside him leaning forward listening to the music. Gold scrollwork and sconces and the tall columnar folds of the drapes at either side of the stage. She held his hand in her lap and he could feel the tops of her stockings through the thin stuff of her summer dress. Freeze this frame. Now call down your dark and your cold and be damned.

He fashioned sweeps from two old brooms he'd found and wired them to the cart to clear the limbs from the road in front of the wheels and he put the boy in the basket and stood on the rear rail like a dogmusher and they set off down the hills, guiding the cart on the curves with their bodies in the manner of bobsledders. It was the first that he'd seen the boy smile in a long time.

At the crest of the hill was a curve and a pullout in the road. An old trail that led off through the woods. They walked out and sat on a bench and looked out over the valley where the land rolled away into the gritty fog. A lake down there. Cold and gray and heavy in the scavenged bowl of the countryside.

What is that, Papa?

It's a dam.

What's it for?

It made the lake. Before they built the dam that was just a river down there. The dam used the water that ran through it to turn big fans called turbines that would generate electricity.

To make lights.

Yes. To make lights.

Can we go down there and see it?

I think it's too far.

Will the dam be there for a long time?

I think so. It's made out of concrete. It will probably be there for hundreds of years. Thousands, even.

Do you think there could be fish in the lake?

No. There's nothing in the lake.

In that long ago somewhere very near this place he'd watched a falcon fall down the long blue wall of the mountain and break with the keel of its breastbone the midmost from a flight of cranes and take it to the river below all gangly and wrecked and trailing its loose and blowsy plumage in the still autumn air.

.   .   .

The grainy air. The taste of it never left your mouth. They stood in the rain like farm animals. Then they went on, holding the tarp over them in the dull drizzle. Their feet were wet and cold and their shoes were being ruined. On the hillsides old crops dead and flattened. The barren ridgeline trees raw and black in the rain.

And the dreams so rich in color. How else would death call you? Waking in the cold dawn it all turned to ash instantly. Like certain ancient frescoes entombed for centuries suddenly exposed to the day.

The weather lifted and the cold and they came at last into the broad lowland river valley, the pieced farmland still visible, everything dead to the root along the barren bottomlands. They trucked on along the blacktop. Tall clapboard houses. Machinerolled metal roofs. A log barn in a field with an advertisement in faded ten-foot letters across the roofslope. See Rock City.

The roadside hedges were gone to rows of black and twisted brambles. No sign of life. He left the boy standing in the road holding the pistol while he climbed an old set of limestone steps and walked down the porch of the farmhouse shading his eyes and peering in the windows. He let himself in through the kitchen. Trash in the floor, old newsprint. China in a breakfront, cups hanging from their hooks. He went down the hallway and stood in the door to the parlor. There was an antique pumporgan in the corner. A television set. Cheap stuffed furniture together with an old handmade cherrywood chifforobe. He climbed the stairs and walked through the bedrooms. Everything covered with ash. A child's room with a stuffed dog on the windowsill looking out at the garden. He went through the closets. He stripped back the beds and came away with two good woolen blankets and went back down the stairs. In the pantry were three jars of homecanned tomatoes. He blew the dust from the lids and studied them. Someone before him had not trusted them and in the end neither did he and he walked out with the blankets over his shoulder and they set off along the road again.

On the outskirts of the city they came to a supermarket. A few old cars in the trashstrewn parking lot. They left the cart in the lot and walked the littered aisles. In the produce section in the bottom of the bins they found a few ancient runner beans and what looked to have once been apricots, long dried to wrinkled effigies of themselves. The boy followed behind. They pushed out through the rear door. In the alleyway behind the store a few shopping carts, all badly rusted. They went back through the store again looking for another cart but there were none. By the door were two softdrink machines that had been tilted over into the floor and opened with a prybar. Coins everywhere in the ash. He sat and ran his hand around in the works of the gutted machines and in the second one it closed over a cold metal cylinder. He withdrew his hand slowly and sat looking at a Coca Cola.

What is it, Papa?

It's a treat. For you.

What is it?

Here. Sit down.

He slipped the boy's knapsack straps loose and set the pack on the floor behind him and he put his thumbnail under the aluminum clip on the top of the can and opened it. He leaned his nose to the slight fizz coming from the can and then handed it to the boy. Go ahead, he said.

The boy took the can. It's bubbly, he said.

Go ahead.

He looked at his father and then tilted the can and drank. He sat there thinking about it. It's really good, he said.

Yes. It is.

You have some, Papa.

I want you to drink it.

You have some.

He took the can and sipped it and handed it back. You drink it, he said. Let's just sit here.

It's because I wont ever get to drink another one, isnt it?

Ever's a long time.

Okay, the boy said.

By dusk of the day following they were at the city. The long concrete sweeps of the interstate exchanges like the ruins of a vast funhouse against the distant murk. He carried the revolver in his belt at the front and wore his parka unzipped. The mummied dead everywhere. The flesh cloven along the bones, the ligaments dried to tug and taut as wires. Shriveled and drawn like latterday bog-folk, their faces of boiled sheeting, the yellowed palings of their teeth. They were discalced to a man like pilgrims of some common order for all their shoes were long since stolen.

They went on. He kept constant watch behind him in the mirror. The only thing that moved in the streets was the blowing ash. They crossed the high concrete bridge over the river. A dock below. Small pleasureboats half sunken in the gray water. Tall stacks downriver dim in the soot.

The day following some few miles south of the city at a bend in the road and half lost in the dead brambles they came upon an old frame house with chimneys and gables and a stone wall. The man stopped. Then he pushed the cart up the drive.

What is this place, Papa?

It's the house where I grew up.

The boy stood looking at it. The peeling wooden clapboards were largely gone from the lower walls for firewood leaving the studs and the insulation exposed. The rotted screening from the back porch lay on the concrete terrace.

Are we going in?

Why not?

I'm scared.

Dont you want to see where I used to live?

No.

It'll be okay.

There could be somebody here.

I dont think so.

But suppose there is?

He stood looking up at the gable to his old room. He looked at the boy. Do you want to wait here?

No. You always say that.

I'm sorry.

I know. But you do.

They slipped out of their backpacks and left them on the terrace and kicked their way through the trash on the porch and pushed into the kitchen. The boy held on to his hand. All much as he'd remembered it. The rooms empty. In the small room off the diningroom there was a bare iron cot, a metal foldingtable. The same castiron coalgrate in the small fireplace. The pine paneling was gone from the walls leaving just the furring strips. He stood there. He felt with his thumb in the painted wood of the mantle the pinholes from tacks that had held stockings forty years ago. This is where we used to have Christmas when I was a boy. He turned and looked out at the waste of the yard. A tangle of dead lilac. The shape of a hedge. On cold winter nights when the electricity was out in a storm we would sit at the fire here, me and my sisters, doing our homework. The boy watched him. Watched shapes claiming him he could not see. We should go, Papa, he said. Yes, the man said. But he didnt.

They walked through the diningroom where the firebrick in the hearth was as yellow as the day it was laid because his mother could not bear to see it blackened. The floor buckled from the rainwater. In the livingroom the bones of a small animal dismembered and placed in a pile. Possibly a cat. A glass tumbler by the door. The boy gripped his hand. They went up the stairs and turned and went down the hallway. Small cones of damp plaster standing in the floor. The wooden lathes of the ceiling exposed. He stood in the doorway to his room. A small space under the eaves. This is where I used to sleep. My cot was against this wall. In the nights in their thousands to dream the dreams of a child's imaginings, worlds rich or fearful such as might offer themselves but never the one to be. He pushed open the closet door half expecting to find his childhood things. Raw cold daylight fell through from the roof. Gray as his heart.

We should go, Papa. Can we go?

Yes. We can go.

I'm scared.

I know. I'm sorry.

I'm really scared.

It's all right. We shouldnt have come.

Three nights later in the foothills of the eastern mountains he woke in the darkness to hear something coming. He lay with his hands at either side of him. The ground was trembling. It was coming toward them.

Papa? The boy said. Papa?

Shh. It's okay.

What is it, Papa?

It neared, growing louder. Everything trembling. Then it passed beneath them like an underground train and drew away into the night and was gone. The boy clung to him crying, his head buried against his chest. Shh. It's all right.

I'm so scared.

I know. It's all right. It's gone.

What was it, Papa?

It was an earthquake. It's gone now. We're all right. Shh.

In those first years the roads were peopled with refugees shrouded up in their clothing. Wearing masks and goggles, sitting in their rags by the side of the road like ruined aviators. Their barrows heaped with shoddy. Towing wagons or carts. Their eyes bright in their skulls. Creedless shells of men tottering down the causeways like migrants in a feverland. The frailty of everything revealed at last. Old and troubling issues resolved into nothingness and night. The last instance of a thing takes the class with it. Turns out the light and is gone. Look around you. Ever is a long time. But the boy knew what he knew. That ever is no time at all.

He sat by a gray window in the gray light in an abandoned house in the late afternoon and read old newspapers while the boy slept. The curious news. The quaint concerns. At eight the primrose closes. He watched the boy sleeping. Can you do it? When the time comes? Can you?

. . .

They squatted in the road and ate cold rice and cold beans that they'd cooked days ago. Already beginning to ferment. No place to make a fire that would not be seen. They slept huddled together in the rank quilts in the dark and the cold. He held the boy close to him. So thin. My heart, he said. My heart. But he knew that if he were a good father still it might well be as she had said. That the boy was all that stood between him and death.

Late in the year. He hardly knew the month. He thought they had enough food to get through the mountains but there was no way to tell. The pass at the watershed was five thousand feet and it was going to be very cold. He said that everything depended on reaching the coast, yet waking in the night he knew that all of this was empty and no substance to it. There was a good chance they would die in the mountains and that would be that.

They passed through the ruins of a resort town and took the road south. Burnt forests for miles along the slopes and snow sooner than he would have thought. No tracks in the road, nothing living anywhere. The fireblackened boulders like the shapes of bears on the starkly wooded slopes. He stood on a stone bridge where the waters slurried into a pool and turned slowly in a gray foam. Where once he'd watched trout swaying in the current, tracking their perfect shadows on the stones beneath. They went on, the boy trudging in his track. Leaning into the cart, winding slowly upward through the switchbacks. There were fires still burning high in the mountains and at night they could see the light from them deep orange in the sootfall. It was getting colder but they had campfires all night and left them burning behind them when they set out again in the morning. He'd wrapped their feet in sacking tied with cord and so far the snow was only a few inches deep but he knew that if it got much deeper they would have to leave the cart. Already it was hard going and he stopped often to rest. Slogging to the edge of the road with his back to the child where he stood bent with his hands on his knees, coughing. He raised up and stood with weeping eyes. On the gray snow a fine mist of blood.

They camped against a boulder and he made a shelter of poles with the tarp. He got a fire going and they set about dragging up a great brushpile of wood to see them through the night. They'd piled a mat of dead hemlock boughs over the snow and they sat wrapped in their blankets watching the fire and drinking the last of the cocoa scavenged weeks before. It was snowing again, soft flakes drifting down out of the blackness. He dozed in the wonderful warmth. The boy's shadow crossed over him. Carrying an armload of wood. He watched him stoke the flames. God's own firedrake. The sparks rushed upward and died in the starless dark. Not all dying words are true and this blessing is no less real for being shorn of its ground.

He woke toward the morning with the fire down to coals and walked out to the road. Everything was alight. As if the lost sun were returning at last. The snow orange and quivering. A forest fire was making its way along the tinderbox ridges above them, flaring and shimmering against the overcast like the northern lights. Cold as it was he stood there a long time. The color of it moved something in him long forgotten. Make a list. Recite a litany. Remember.

It was colder. Nothing moved in that high world. A rich smell of woodsmoke hung over the road. He pushed the cart on through the snow. A few miles each day. He'd no notion how far the summit might be. They ate sparely and they were hungry all the time. He stood looking out over the country. A river far below. How far had they come?

In his dream she was sick and he cared for her. The dream bore the look of sacrifice but he thought differently. He did not take care of her and she died alone somewhere in the dark and there is no other dream nor other waking world and there is no other tale to tell.

On this road there are no godspoke men. They are gone and I am left and they have taken with them the world. Query: How does the never to be differ from what never was?

Dark of the invisible moon. The nights now only slightly less black. By day the banished sun circles the earth like a grieving mother with a lamp.

People sitting on the sidewalk in the dawn half immolate and smoking in their clothes. Like failed sectarian suicides. Others would come to help them. Within a year there were fires on the ridges and deranged chanting. The screams of the murdered. By day the dead impaled on spikes along the road. What had they done? He thought that in the history of the world it might even be that there was more punishment than crime but he took small comfort from it.

The air grew thin and he thought the summit could not be far. Perhaps tomorrow. Tomorrow came and went. It didnt snow again but the snow in the road was six inches deep and pushing the cart up those grades was exhausting work. He thought they would have to leave it. How much could they carry? He stood and looked out over the barren slopes. The ash fell on the snow till it was all but black.

At every curve it looked as though the pass lay just ahead and then one evening he stopped and looked all about and he recognized it. He unsnapped the throat of his parka and lowered the hood and stood listening. The wind in the dead black stands of hemlock. The empty parking lot at the overlook. The boy stood beside him. Where he'd stood

33

once with his own father in a winter long ago. What is it, Papa? the boy said.

It's the gap. This is it.

In the morning they pressed on. It was very cold. Toward the afternoon it began to snow again and they made camp early and crouched under the leanto of the tarp and watched the snow fall in the fire. By morning there was several inches of new snow on the ground but the snow had stopped and it was so quiet they could all but hear their hearts. He piled wood on the coals and fanned the fire to life and trudged out through the drifts to dig out the cart. He sorted through the cans and went back and they sat by the fire and ate the last of their crackers and a tin of sausage. In a pocket of his knapsack he'd found a last half packet of cocoa and he fixed it for the boy and then poured his own cup with hot water and sat blowing at the rim.

You promised not to do that, the boy said.

What?

You know what, Papa.

He poured the hot water back into the pan and took the boy's cup and poured some of the cocoa into his own and then handed it back.

I have to watch you all the time, the boy said.

I know.

If you break little promises you'll break big ones. That's what you said.

I know. But I wont.

They slogged all day down the southfacing slope of the watershed. In the deeper drifts the cart wouldnt push at all and he had to drag it behind him with one hand while he broke trail. Anywhere but in the mountains they might have found something to use for a sled. An old metal sign or a sheet of roofingtin. The wrappings on their feet had soaked through and they were cold and wet all day. He leaned on the cart to get his breath while the boy waited. There was a sharp crack from somewhere on the mountain. Then another. It's just a tree falling, he said. It's okay. The boy was looking at the dead roadside trees. It's okay, the man said. All the trees in the world are going to fall sooner or later. But not on us.

How do you know?

I just know.

. . .

Still they came to trees across the road where they were forced to unload the cart and carry everything over the trunks and then repack it all on the far side. The boy found toys he'd forgot he had. He kept out a yellow truck and they went on with it sitting on top of the tarp.

They camped in a bench of land on the far side of a frozen roadside creek. The wind had blown the ash from the ice and the ice was black and the creek looked like a path of basalt winding through the woods. They collected firewood from the north side of the slope where it was not so wet, pushing over whole trees and dragging them into camp. They got the fire going and spread their tarp and hung their wet clothes on poles to steam and stink and they sat wrapped in the quilts naked while the man held the boy's feet against his stomach to warm them.

He woke whimpering in the night and the man held him. Shh, he said. Shh. It's okay.

I had a bad dream.

I know.

Should I tell you what it was?

If you want to.

I had this penguin that you wound up and it would waddle and flap its flippers. And we were in that house that we used to live in and it came around the corner but nobody had wound it up and it was really scary.

Okay.

It was a lot scarier in the dream.

I know. Dreams can be really scary.

Why did I have that scary dream?

I dont know. But it's okay now. I'm going to put some wood on the fire. You go to sleep.

The boy didnt answer. Then he said: The winder wasnt turning.

It took four more days to come down out of the snow and even then there were patches of snow in certain bends of the road and the road was black and wet from the up-country runoff even beyond that. They came out along the rim of a deep gorge and far down in the darkness a river. They stood listening.

High rock bluffs on the far side of the canyon with thin black trees clinging to the escarpment. The sound of the river faded. Then it returned. A cold wind blowing up from the country below. They were all day reaching the river.

They left the cart in a parking area and walked out through the woods. A low thunder coming from the river. It was a waterfall dropping off a high shelf of rock and falling eighty feet through a gray shroud of mist into the pool below. They could smell the water and they could feel the cold coming off of it. A bench of wet river gravel. He stood and watched the boy. Wow, the boy said. He couldnt take his eyes off it.

He squatted and scooped up a handful of stones and smelled them and let them fall clattering. Polished round and smooth as marbles or lozenges of stone veined and striped. Black disclets and bits of polished quartz all bright from the mist off the river. The boy walked out and squatted and laved up the dark water.

The waterfall fell into the pool almost at its center. A gray curd circled. They stood side by side calling to each other over the din.

Is it cold?

Yes. It's freezing.

Do you want to go in?

I dont know.

Sure you do.

Is it okay?

Come on.

He unzipped his parka and let it fall to the gravel and the boy stood up and they undressed and walked out into the water. Ghostly pale and shivering. The boy so thin it stopped his heart. He dove headlong and came up gasping and turned and stood, beating his arms.

Is it over my head? the boy called.

No. Come on.

He turned and swam out to the falls and let the water beat upon him. The boy was standing in the pool to his waist, holding his shoulders and hopping up and down. The man went back and got him. He held him and floated him about, the boy gasping and chopping at the water. You're doing good, the man said. You're doing good.

They dressed shivering and then climbed the trail to the upper river. They walked out along the rocks to where the river seemed to end in space and he held the boy while he ventured out to the last ledge of rock. The river went sucking over the rim and fell straight down into the pool below. The entire river. He clung to the man's arm.

It's really far, he said.

It's pretty far.

Would you die if you fell?

You'd get hurt. It's a long way.

It's really scary.

They walked out through the woods. The light was failing. They followed the flats along the upper river among huge dead trees. A rich southern wood that once held mayapple and pipsissewa. Ginseng. The raw dead limbs of the rhododendron twisted and knotted and black. He stopped. Something in the mulch and ash. He stooped and cleared it away. A small colony of them, shrunken, dried and wrinkled. He picked one and held it up and sniffed it. He bit a piece from the edge and chewed.

What is it, Papa?

Morels. It's morels.

What's morels?

They're a kind of mushroom.

Can you eat them?

Yes. Take a bite.

Are they good?

Take a bite.

The boy smelled the mushroom and bit into it and stood chewing. He looked at his father. These are pretty good, he said.

They pulled the morels from the ground, small alien-looking things that he piled in the hood of the boy's parka. They hiked back out to the road and down to where they'd left the cart and they made camp by the river pool at the falls and washed the earth and ash from the morels and put them to soak in a pan of water. By the time he had the fire going it was dark and he sliced a handful of the mushrooms on a log for their dinner and scooped them into the frying pan along with the fat pork from a can of beans and set them in the coals to simmer. The boy watched him. This is a good place Papa, he said.

They ate the little mushrooms together with the beans and drank tea and had tinned pears for their desert. He banked the fire against the seam of rock where he'd built it and he strung the tarp behind them to reflect the heat and they sat warm in their refuge while he told the boy stories. Old stories of courage and justice as he remembered them until the boy was asleep in his blankets and then he stoked the fire and lay down warm and full and listened to the low thunder of the falls beyond them in that dark and threadbare wood.

He walked out in the morning and took the river path downstream. The boy was right that it was a good place and he wanted to check for any sign of other visitors. He found nothing. He stood watching the river where it swung loping into a pool and curled and eddied. He dropped a white stone into the water but it vanished as suddenly as if it had been eaten. He'd stood at such a river once and watched the flash of trout deep in a pool, invisible to see in the teacolored water except as they turned on their sides to feed. Reflecting back the sun deep in the darkness like a flash of knives in a cave.

We cant stay, he said. It's getting colder every day. And the waterfall is an attraction. It was for us and it will be for others and we dont know who they will be and we cant hear them coming. It's not safe.

We could stay one more day.

It's not safe.

Well maybe we could find some other place on the river.

We have to keep moving. We have to keep heading south.

Doesnt the river go south?

No. It doesnt.

Can I see it on the map?

Yes. Let me get it.

The tattered oilcompany roadmap had once been taped together but now it was just sorted into leaves and numbered with crayon in the corners for their assembly. He sorted through the limp pages and spread out those that answered to their location.

We cross a bridge here. It looks to be about eight miles or so. This is the river. Going east. We follow the road here along the eastern slope of the mountains. These are our roads, the black lines on the map. The state roads.

Why are they the state roads?

Because they used to belong to the states. What used to be called the states.

But there's not any more states?

No.

What happened to them?

I dont know exactly. That's a good question.

But the roads are still there.

Yes. For a while.

How long a while?

I dont know. Maybe quite a while. There's nothing to uproot them so they should be okay for a while.

But there wont be any cars or trucks on them.

No.

Okay.

Are you ready?

The boy nodded. He wiped his nose on his sleeve and shouldered up his small pack and the man folded away the map sections and rose and the boy followed him out through the gray palings of the trees to the road.

When the bridge came in sight below them there was a tractor-trailer jackknifed sideways across it and wedged into the buckled iron railings. It was raining again and they stood there with the rain pattering softly on the tarp. Peering out from under the blue gloom beneath the plastic.

Can we get around it? the boy said.

I dont think so. We can probably get under it. We may have to unload the cart.

The bridge spanned the river above a rapids. They could hear the noise of it as they came around the curve in the road. A wind was coming down the gorge and they pulled the corners of the tarp about them and pushed the cart out onto the bridge. They could see the river through the ironwork. Below the rapids was a railroad bridge laid on limestone piers. The stones of the piers were stained well above the river from the high water and the bend of the river was choked with great windrows of black limbs and brush and the trunks of trees.

The truck had been there for years, the tires flat and crumpled under the rims. The front of the tractor was jammed against the railing of the bridge and the trailer had sheared forward off the top plate and jammed up against the back of the cab. The rear of the trailer had swung out and buckled the rail on the other side of the bridge and it hung several feet out over the river gorge. He pushed the cart up under the trailer but the handle wouldnt clear. They'd have to slide it under sideways. He left it sitting in the rain with the tarp over it and they duckwalked under the trailer and he left the boy crouched there in the dry while he climbed up on the gastank step and wiped the water from the glass and peered inside the cab. He stepped back down and reached up and opened the door and then climbed in and pulled the door shut behind him. He sat looking around. An old doghouse sleeper behind the seats. Papers in the floor. The glovebox was open but it was empty. He climbed back between the seats. There was a raw damp mattress on the bunk and a small refrigerator with the door standing open. A fold-down table. Old magazines in the floor. He went through the plywood lockers overhead but they were empty. There were drawers under the bunk and he pulled them out and looked through the trash. He climbed forward into the cab again and sat in the driver's seat and looked out down the river through the slow trickle of water on the glass. The thin drum of rain on the metal roof and the slow darkness falling over everything.

They slept that night in the truck and in the morning the rain had stopped and they unloaded the cart and passed everything under the truck to the other side and reloaded it. Down the bridge a hundred feet or so were the blackened remains of tires that had been burned there. He stood looking at the trailer. What do you think is in there? he said.

I dont know.

We're not the first ones here. So probably nothing.

There's no way to get in.

He put his ear to the side of the trailer and whacked the sheetmetal with the flat of his hand. It sounds empty, he said. You can probably get in from the roof. Somebody would have cut a hole in the side of it by now.

What would they cut it with?

They'd find something.

He took off his parka and laid it across the top of the cart and climbed on to the fender of the tractor and on to the hood and clambered up over the windscreen to the roof of the cab. He stood and turned and looked down at the river. Wet metal underfoot. He looked down at the boy. The boy looked worried. He turned and reached and got a grip on the front of the trailer and slowly pulled himself up. It was all he could do and there was a lot less of him to pull. He got one leg up over the edge and hung there resting. Then he pulled himself up and rolled over and sat up.

There was a skylight about a third of the way down the roof and he made his way to it in a walking crouch. The cover was gone and the inside of the trailer smelled of wet plywood and that sour smell he'd come to know. He had a magazine in his hip pocket and he took it out and tore some pages from it and wadded them and got out his lighter and lit the papers and dropped them into the darkness. A faint whooshing. He wafted away the smoke and looked down into the trailer. The small fire burning in the floor seemed a long way down. He shielded the glare of it with his hand and when he did he could see almost to the rear of the box. Human bodies. Sprawled in every attitude. Dried and shrunken in their rotted clothes. The small wad of burning paper drew down to a wisp of flame and then died out leaving a faint pattern for just a moment in the incandescence like the shape of a flower, a molten rose. Then all was dark again.

They camped that night in the woods on a ridge overlooking the broad piedmont plain where it stretched away to the south. He built a cookfire against a rock and they ate the last of the morels and a can of spinach. In the night a storm broke in the mountains above them and came cannonading downcountry cracking and booming and the stark gray world appeared again and again out of the night in the shrouded flare of the lightning. The boy clung to him. It all passed on. A brief rattle of hail and then the slow cold rain.

When he woke again it was still dark but the rain had stopped. A smoky light out there in the valley. He rose and walked out along the ridge. A haze of fire that stretched for miles. He squatted and watched it. He could smell the smoke. He wet his finger and held it to the wind. When he rose and turned to go back the tarp was lit from within where the boy had wakened. Sited there in the darkness the frail blue shape of it looked like the pitch of some last venture at the edge of the world. Something all but unaccountable. And so it was.

All the day following they traveled through the drifting haze of woodsmoke. In the draws the smoke coming off the ground like mist and the thin black trees burning on the slopes like stands of heathen candles. Late in the day they came to a place where the fire had crossed the road and the macadam was still warm and further on it began to soften underfoot. The hot black mastic sucking at their shoes and stretching in thin bands as they stepped. They stopped. We'll have to wait, he said.

They backtracked and camped in the actual road and when they went on in the morning the macadam had cooled. Bye and bye they came to a set of tracks cooked into the tar. They just suddenly appeared. He squatted and studied them. Someone had come out of the woods in the night and continued down the melted roadway.

Who is it? said the boy.

I dont know. Who is anybody?

They came upon him shuffling along the road before them, dragging one leg slightly and stopping from time to time to stand stooped and uncertain before setting out again.

What should we do, Papa?

We're all right. Let's just follow and watch.

Take a look, the boy said.

Yes. Take a look.

They followed him a good ways but at his pace they were losing the day and finally he just sat in the road and did not get up again. The boy hung on to his father's coat. No one spoke. He was as burntlooking as the country, his clothing scorched and black. One of his eyes was burnt shut and his hair was but a nitty wig of ash upon his blackened skull. As they passed he looked down. As if he'd done something wrong. His shoes were bound up with wire and coated with roadtar and he sat there in silence, bent over in his rags. The boy kept looking back. Papa? he whispered. What is wrong with the man?

He's been struck by lightning.

Cant we help him? Papa?

No. We cant help him.

The boy kept pulling at his coat. Papa? he said.

Stop it.

Cant we help him Papa?

No. We cant help him. There's nothing to be done for him.

. . .

They went on. The boy was crying. He kept looking back. When they got to the bottom of the hill the man stopped and looked at him and looked back up the road. The burned man had fallen over and at that distance you couldnt even tell what it was. I'm sorry, he said. But we have nothing to give him. We have no way to help him. I'm sorry for what happened to him but we cant fix it. You know that, dont you? The boy stood looking down. He nodded his head. Then they went on and he didnt look back again.

At evening a dull sulphur light from the fires. The standing water in the roadside ditches black with the runoff. The mountains shrouded away. They crossed a river by a concrete bridge where skeins of ash and slurry moved slowly in the current. Charred bits of wood. In the end they stopped and turned back and camped under the bridge.

He'd carried his billfold about till it wore a cornershaped hole in his trousers. Then one day he sat by the roadside and took it out and went through the contents. Some money, credit cards. His driver's license. A picture of his wife. He spread everything out on the blacktop. Like gaming cards. He pitched the sweatblackened piece of leather into the woods and sat holding the photograph. Then he laid it down in the road also and then he stood and they went on.

In the morning he lay looking up at the clay nests that swallows had built in the corners under the bridge. He looked at the boy but the boy had turned away and lay staring out at the river.

There's nothing we could have done.

He didnt answer.

He's going to die. We cant share what we have or we'll die too.

I know.

So when are you going to talk to me again?

I'm talking now.

Are you sure?

Yes.

Okay.

Okay.

. . .

They stood on the far shore of a river and called to him. Tattered gods slouching in their rags across the waste. Trekking the dried floor of a mineral sea where it lay cracked and broken like a fallen plate. Paths of feral fire in the coagulate sands. The figures faded in the distance. He woke and lay in the dark.

The clocks stopped at 1:17. A long shear of light and then a series of low concussions. He got up and went to the window. What is it? she said. He didnt answer. He went into the bathroom and threw the lightswitch but the power was already gone. A dull rose glow in the windowglass. He dropped to one knee and raised the lever to stop the tub and then turned on both taps as far as they would go. She was standing in the doorway in her nightwear, clutching the jamb, cradling her belly in one hand. What is it? she said. What is happening?

I dont know.

Why are you taking a bath?

I'm not.

Once in those early years he'd wakened in a barren wood and lay listening to flocks of migratory birds overhead in that bitter dark. Their half muted crankings miles above where they circled the earth as senselessly as insects trooping the rim of a bowl. He wished them godspeed till they were gone. He never heard them again.

He'd a deck of cards he found in a bureau drawer in a house and the cards were worn and spindled and the two of clubs was missing but still they played sometimes by firelight wrapped in their blankets. He tried to remember the rules of childhood games. Old Maid. Some version of Whist. He was sure he had them mostly wrong and he made up new games and gave them made up names. Abnormal Fescue or Catbarf. Sometimes the child would ask him questions about the world that for him was not even a memory. He thought hard how to answer. There is no past. What would you like? But he stopped making things up because those things were not true either and the telling made him feel bad. The child had his own fantasies. How things would be in the south. Other children. He tried to keep a rein on this but his heart was not in it. Whose would be?

. . .

No lists of things to be done. The day providential to itself. The hour. There is no later. This is later. All things of grace and beauty such that one holds them to one's heart have a common provenance in pain. Their birth in grief and ashes. So, he whispered to the sleeping boy. I have you.

He thought about the picture in the road and he thought that he should have tried to keep her in their lives in some way but he didnt know how. He woke coughing and walked out so as not to wake the child. Following a stone wall in the dark, wrapped in his blanket, kneeling in the ashes like a penitent. He coughed till he could taste the blood and he said her name aloud. He thought perhaps he'd said it in his sleep. When he got back the boy was awake. I'm sorry, he said.

It's okay.

Go to sleep.

I wish I was with my mom.

He didnt answer. He sat beside the small figure wrapped in the quilts and blankets. After a while he said: You mean you wish that you were dead.

Yes.

You musnt say that.

But I do.

Dont say it. It's a bad thing to say.

I cant help it.

I know. But you have to.

How do I do it?

I dont know.

We're survivors he told her across the flame of the lamp.

Survivors? she said.

Yes.

What in God's name are you talking about? We're not survivors. We're the walking dead in a horror film.

I'm begging you.

I dont care. I dont care if you cry. It doesnt mean anything to me.

Please.

Stop it.

I am begging you. I'll do anything.

Such as what? I should have done it a long time ago. When there were three bullets in the gun instead of two. I was stupid. We've been over all of this. I didnt bring myself to this. I was brought. And now I'm done. I thought about not even telling you. That would probably have been best. You have two bullets and then what? You cant protect us. You say you would die for us but what good is that? I'd take him with me if it werent for you. You know I would. It's the right thing to do.

You're talking crazy.

No, I'm speaking the truth. Sooner or later they will catch us and they will kill us. They will rape me. They'll rape him. They are going to rape us and kill us and eat us and you wont face it. You'd rather wait for it to happen. But I cant. I cant. She sat there smoking a slender length of dried grapevine as if it were some rare cheroot. Holding it with a certain elegance, her other hand across her knees where she'd drawn them up. She watched him across the small flame. We used to talk about death, she said. We dont any more. Why is that?

I dont know.

It's because it's here. There's nothing left to talk about.

I wouldnt leave you.

I dont care. It's meaningless. You can think of me as a faithless slut if you like. I've taken a new lover. He can give me what you cannot.

Death is not a lover.

Oh yes he is.

Please dont do this.

I'm sorry.

I cant do it alone.

Then dont. I cant help you. They say that women dream of danger to those in their care and men of danger to themselves. But I dont dream at all. You say you cant? Then dont do it. That's all. Because I am done with my own whorish heart and I have been for a long time. You talk about taking a stand but there is no stand to take. My heart was ripped out of me the night he was born so dont ask for sorrow now. There is none. Maybe you'll be good at this. I doubt it, but who knows. The one thing I can tell you is that you wont survive for yourself. I know because I would never have come this far. A person who had no one would be well advised to cobble together some passable ghost. Breathe it into being and coax it along with words of love. Offer it each phantom crumb and shield it from harm with your body. As for me my only hope is for eternal nothingness and I hope it with all my heart.

He didnt answer.

You have no argument because there is none.

Will you tell him goodbye?

No. I will not.

Just wait till morning. Please.

I have to go.

She had already stood up.

For the love of God, woman. What am I to tell him?

I cant help you.

Where are you going to go? You cant even see.

I dont have to.

He stood up. I'm begging you, he said.

No. I will not. I cannot.

She was gone and the coldness of it was her final gift. She would do it with a flake of obsidian. He'd taught her himself. Sharper than steel. The edge an atom thick. And she was right. There was no argument. The hundred nights they'd sat up arguing the pros and cons of self destruction with the earnestness of philosophers chained to a madhouse wall. In the morning the boy said nothing at all and when they were packed and ready to set out upon the road he turned and looked back at their campsite and he said: She's gone isn't she? And he said: Yes, she is.

Always so deliberate, hardly surprised by the most out-landish advents. A creation perfectly evolved to meet its own end. They sat at the window and ate in their robes by candlelight a midnight supper and watched distant cities burn. A few nights later she gave birth in their bed by the light of a drycell lamp. Gloves meant for dishwashing. The improbable appearance of the small crown of the head. Streaked with blood and lank black hair. The rank meconium. Her cries meant nothing to him. Beyond the window just the gathering cold, the fires on the horizon. He held aloft the scrawny red body so raw and naked and cut the cord with kitchen shears and wrapped his son in a towel.

Did you have any friends?
Yes. I did.
Lots of them?
Yes.
Do you remember them?
Yes. I remember them.
What happened to them?
They died.
All of them?
Yes. All of them.
Do you miss them?

Yes. I do.

Where are we going?

We're going south.

Okay.

They were all day on the long black road, stopping in the afternoon to eat sparingly from their meager supplies. The boy took his truck from the pack and shaped roads in the ash with a stick. The truck tooled along slowly. He made truck noises. The day seemed almost warm and they slept in the leaves with their packs under their heads.

Something woke him. He turned on his side and lay listening. He raised his head slowly, the pistol in his hand. He looked down at the boy and when he looked back toward the road the first of them were already coming into view. God, he whispered. He reached and shook the boy, keeping his eyes on the road. They came shuffling through the ash casting their hooded heads from side to side. Some of them wearing canister masks. One in a biohazard suit. Stained and filthy. Slouching along with clubs in their hands, lengths of pipe. Coughing. Then he heard on the road behind them what sounded like a diesel truck. Quick, he whispered. Quick. He shoved the pistol in his belt and grabbed the boy by the hand and he dragged the cart through the trees and tilted it over where it would not so easily be seen. The boy was frozen with fear. He pulled him to him. It's all right, he said. We have to run. Dont look back. Come on.

He slung their knapsacks over his shoulder and they tore through the crumbling bracken. The boy was terrified. Run, he whispered. Run. He looked back. The truck had rumbled into view. Men standing in the bed looking out. The boy fell and he pulled him up. It's all right, he said. Come on.

He could see a break through the trees that he thought was a ditch or a cut and they came out through the weeds into an old roadway. Plates of cracked macadam showing through the drifts of ash. He pulled the boy down and they crouched under the bank listening, gasping for breath. They could hear the diesel engine out on the road, running on God knows what. When he raised up to look he could just see the top of the truck moving along the road. Men standing in the stakebed, some of them holding rifles. The truck passed on and the black diesel smoke coiled through the woods. The motor sounded ropy. Missing and puttering. Then it quit.

He sank down and put his hand on top of his head. God, he said. They could hear the thing rattle and flap to a halt. Then just the silence. He had the pistol in his hand, he couldnt even remember taking it from his belt. They could hear the men talking. Hear them unlatch and raise the hood. He sat with his arm around the boy. Shh, he said. Shh. After a while they heard the truck begin to roll. Lumbering and creaking like a ship. They'd have no other way to start it save to push it and they couldnt get it fast enough to start on that slope. After a few minutes it coughed and bucked and stopped again. He raised his head to look and coming through the weeds twenty feet away was one of their number unbuckling his belt. They both froze.

. . .

64

He cocked the pistol and held it on the man and the man stood with one hand out at his side, the dirty crumpled paintmask that he wore sucking in and out.

Just keep coming.

He looked at the road.

Dont look back there. Look at me. If you call out you're dead.

He came forward, holding his belt by one hand. The holes in it marked the progress of his emaciation and the leather at one side had a lacquered look to it where he was used to stropping the blade of his knife. He stepped down into the roadcut and he looked at the gun and he looked at the boy. Eyes collared in cups of grime and deeply sunk. Like an animal inside a skull looking out the eyeholes. He wore a beard that had been cut square across the bottom with shears and he had a tattoo of a bird on his neck done by someone with an illformed notion of their appearance. He was lean, wiry, rachitic. Dressed in a pair of filthy blue coveralls and a black billcap with the logo of some vanished enterprise embroidered across the front of it.

Where are you going?

I was going to take a crap.

Where are you going with the truck.

I dont know.

What do you mean you dont know? Take the mask off.

He pulled the mask off over his head and stood holding it.

I mean I dont know, he said.

You dont know where you're going?

No.

What's the truck running on.

Diesel fuel.

How much do you have.

There's three fifty-five gallon drums in the bed.

Do you have ammunition for those guns?

He looked back toward the road.

I told you not to look back there.

Yeah. We got ammunition.

Where did you get it?

Found it.

That's a lie. What are you eating.

Whatever we can find.

Whatever you can find.

Yeah. He looked at the boy. You wont shoot, he said.

That's what you think.

You aint got but two shells. Maybe just one. And they'll hear the shot.

Yes they will. But you wont.

66

How do you figure that?

Because the bullet travels faster than sound. It will be in your brain before you can hear it. To hear it you will need a frontal lobe and things with names like colliculus and temporal gyrus and you wont have them anymore. They'll just be soup.

Are you a doctor?

I'm not anything.

We got a man hurt. It'd be worth your while.

Do I look like an imbecile to you?

I dont know what you look like.

Why are you looking at him?

I can look where I want to.

No you cant. If you look at him again I'll shoot you.

The boy was sitting with both hands on top of his head and looking out between his forearms.

I'll bet that boy is hungry. Why dont you all just come on to the truck? Get something to eat. Aint no need to be such a hard-ass.

You dont have anything to eat. Let's go.

Go where?

Let's go.

I aint goin nowheres.

You're not?

No. I aint.

You think I wont kill you but you're wrong. But what I'd rather do is take you up this road a mile or so and then turn you loose. That's all the head start we need. You wont find us. You wont even know which way we went.

You know what I think?

What do you think.

I think you're chickenshit.

He let go of the belt and it fell in the roadway with the gear hanging from it. A canteen. An old canvas army pouch. A leather sheath for a knife. When he looked up the roadrat was holding the knife in his hand. He'd only taken two steps but he was almost between him and the child.

What do you think you're going to do with that?

He didnt answer. He was a big man but he was very quick. He dove and grabbed the boy and rolled and came up holding him against his chest with the knife at his throat. The man had already dropped to the ground and he swung with him and leveled the pistol and fired from a two-handed position balanced on both knees at a distance of six feet. The man fell back instantly and lay with blood bubbling from the hole in his forehead. The boy was lying in his lap with no expression on his face at all. He shoved the pistol in his belt and slung the knapsack over his shoulder and picked up the boy and turned him around and lifted him over his head and set him on his shoulders and set off up the old roadway at a dead run, holding the boy's knees, the boy clutching his forehead, covered with gore and mute as a stone.

They came to an old iron bridge in the woods where the vanished road had crossed an all but vanished stream. He was starting to cough and he'd hardly breath to do it with. He dropped down out of the roadway and into the woods. He turned and stood gasping, trying to listen. He heard nothing. He staggered on another half mile or so and finally dropped to his knees and put the boy down in the ashes and leaves. He wiped the blood from his face and held him. It's okay, he said. It's okay.

In the long cold evening with the darkness dropping down he heard them only once. He held the boy close. There was a cough in his throat that never left. The boy so frail and thin through his coat, shivering like a dog.

The footsteps in the leaves stopped. Then they moved on. They neither spoke nor called to each other, the more sinister for that. With the final onset of dark the iron cold locked down and the boy by now was shuddering violently. No moon rose beyond the murk and there was nowhere to go. They had a single blanket in the pack and he got it out and covered the boy with it and he unzipped his parka and held the boy against him. They lay there for a long time but they were freezing and finally he sat up. We've got to move, he said. We cant just lie here. He looked around but there was nothing to see. He spoke into a blackness without depth or dimension.

He held the boy's hand as they stumbled through the woods. The other hand he held out before him. He could see no worse with his eyes shut. The boy was wrapped in the blanket and he told him not to drop it because they would never find it again. He wanted to be carried but the man told him that he had to keep moving. They stumbled and fell through the woods the night long and long before dawn the boy fell and would not get up again. He wrapped him in his own parka and wrapped him in the blanket and sat holding him, rocking back and forth. A single round left in the revolver. You will not face the truth. You will not.

In the grudging light that passed for day he put the boy in the leaves and sat studying the woods. When it was a bit lighter he rose and walked out and cut a perimeter about their siwash camp looking for sign but other than their own faint track through the ash he saw nothing. He went back and gathered the boy up. We have to go, he said. The boy sat slumped, his face blank. The filth dried in his hair and his face streaked with it. Talk to me, he said, but he would not.

They moved on east through the standing dead trees. They passed an old frame house and crossed a dirt road. A cleared plot of ground perhaps once a truckgarden. Stopping from time to time to listen. The unseen sun cast no shadow. They came upon the road unexpectedly and he stopped the boy with one hand and they crouched in the roadside ditch like lepers and listened. No wind. Dead silence. After a while he rose and walked out into the road. He looked back at the boy. Come on, he said. The boy came out and the man pointed out the tracks in the ash where the truck had gone. The boy stood wrapped in the blanket looking down at the road.

He'd no way to know if they'd got the truck running again. No way to know how long they might be willing to lie in ambush. He thumbed the pack down off his shoulder and sat and opened it. We need to eat, he said. Are you hungry?

The boy shook his head.

No. Of course not. He took out the plastic bottle of water and unscrewed the cap and held it out and the boy took it and stood drinking. He lowered the bottle and got his breath and he sat in the road and crossed his legs and drank again. Then he handed the bottle back and the man drank and screwed the cap back on and rummaged through the pack. They ate a can of white beans, passing it between them, and he threw the empty tin into the woods. Then they set out down the road again.

The truck people had camped in the road itself. They'd built a fire there and charred billets of wood lay stuck in the melted tar together with ash and bones. He squatted and held his hand over the tar. A faint warmth coming off of it. He stood and looked down the road. Then he took the boy with him into the woods. I want you to wait here, he said. I wont be far away. I'll be able to hear you if you call.

Take me with you, the boy said. He looked as if he was going to cry.

No. I want you to wait here.

Please, Papa.

Stop it. I want you to do what I say. Take the gun.

I dont want the gun.

I didnt ask you if you wanted it. Take it.

He walked out through the woods to where they'd left the cart. It was still lying there but it had been plundered. The few things they hadnt taken scattered in the leaves. Some books and toys belonging to the boy. His old shoes and some rags of clothing. He righted the cart and put the boy's things in it and wheeled it out to the road. Then he went back. There was nothing there. Dried blood dark in the leaves. The boy's knapsack was gone. Coming back he found the bones and the skin piled together with rocks over them. A pool of guts. He pushed at the bones with the toe of his shoe. They looked to have been boiled. No pieces of clothing. Dark was coming on again and it was already very cold and he turned and went out to where he'd left the boy and knelt and put his arms around him and held him.

They pushed the cart through the woods as far as the old road and left it there and headed south along the road hurrying against the dark. The boy was stumbling he was so tired and the man picked him up and swung him onto his shoulders and they went on. By the time they got to the bridge there was scarcely light at all. He put the boy down and they felt their way down the embankment. Under the bridge he got out his lighter and lit it and swept the ground with the flickering light. Sand and gravel washed up from the creek. He set down the knapsack and put away the lighter and took hold of the boy by the shoulders. He could just make him out in the darkness. I want you to wait here, he said. I'm going for wood. We have to have a fire.

I'm scared.

I know. But I'll just be a little ways and I'll be able to hear you so if you get scared you call me and I'll come right away.

I'm really scared.

The sooner I go the sooner I'll be back and we'll have a fire and then you wont be scared anymore. Dont lie down. If you lie down you'll fall asleep and then if I call you you wont answer and I wont be able to find you. Do you understand?

The boy didnt answer. He was close to losing his temper with him and then he realized that he was shaking his head in the dark. Okay, he said. Okay.

He scrambled up the bank and into the woods, holding his hands out in front of him. There was wood everwhere, dead limbs and branches scattered over the ground. He shuffled along kicking them into a pile and when he had an armful he stooped and gathered them up and called the boy and the boy answered and talked him back to the bridge. They sat in the darkness while he shaved sticks into a pile with his knife and broke up the small branches with his hands. He took the lighter from his pocket and struck the wheel with his thumb. He used gasoline in the lighter and it burned with a frail blue flame and he bent and set the tinder alight and watched the fire climb upward through the wicker of limbs. He piled on more wood and bent and blew gently at the base of the little blaze and arranged the wood with his hands, shaping the fire just so.

He made two more trips into the woods, dragging arm-loads of brush and limbs to the bridge and pushing them over the side. He could see the glow of the fire from some distance but he didnt think it could be seen from the other road. Below the bridge he could make out a dark pool of standing water among the rocks. A rim of shelving ice. He stood on the bridge and shoved the last pile of wood over, his breath white in the glow of the firelight.

He sat in the sand and inventoried the contents of the knapsack. The binoculars. A half pint bottle of gasoline almost full. The bottle of water. A pair of pliers. Two spoons. He set everything out in a row. There were five small tins of food and he chose a can of sausages and one of corn and he opened these with the little army can opener and set them at the edge of the fire and they sat watching the labels char and curl. When the corn began to steam he took the cans from the fire with the pliers and they sat bent over them with their spoons, eating slowly. The boy was nodding with sleep.

When they'd eaten he took the boy out on the gravelbar below the bridge and he pushed away the thin shore ice with a stick and they knelt there while he washed the boy's face and his hair. The water was so cold the boy was crying. They moved down the gravel to find fresh water and he washed his hair again as well as he could and finally stopped because the boy was moaning with the cold of it. He dried him with the blanket, kneeling there in the glow of the light with the shadow of the bridge's understructure broken across the palisade of treetrunks beyond the creek. This is my child, he said. I wash a dead man's brains out of his hair. That is my job. Then he wrapped him in the blanket and carried him to the fire.

The boy sat tottering. The man watched him that he not topple into the flames. He kicked holes in the sand for the boy's hips and shoulders where he would sleep and he sat holding him while he tousled his hair before the fire to dry it. All of this like some ancient anointing. So be it. Evoke the forms. Where you've nothing else construct ceremonies out of the air and breathe upon them.

He woke in the night with the cold and rose and broke up more wood for the fire. The shapes of the small treelimbs burning incandescent orange in the coals. He blew the flames to life and piled on the wood and sat with his legs crossed, leaning against the stone pier of the bridge. Heavy limestone blocks laid up without mortar. Overhead the ironwork brown with rust, the hammered rivets, the wooden sleepers and crossplanks. The sand where he sat was warm to the touch but the night beyond the fire was sharp with the cold. He got up and dragged fresh wood in under the bridge. He stood listening. The boy didnt stir. He sat beside him and stroked his pale and tangled hair. Golden chalice, good to house a god. Please dont tell me how the story ends. When he looked out again at the darkness beyond the bridge it was snowing.

All the wood they had to burn was small wood and the fire was good for no more than an hour or perhaps a bit more. He dragged the rest of the brush in under the bridge and broke it up, standing on the limbs and cracking them to length. He thought the noise would wake the boy but it didnt. The wet wood hissed in the flames, the snow continued to fall. In the morning they would see if there were tracks in the road or not. This was the first human being other than the boy that he'd spoken to in more than a year. My brother at last. The reptilian calculations in those cold and shifting eyes. The gray and rotting teeth. Claggy with human flesh. Who has made of the world a lie every word. When he woke again the snow had stopped and the grainy dawn was shaping out the naked woodlands beyond the bridge, the trees black against the snow. He was lying curled up with his hands between his knees and he sat up and got the fire going and he set a can of beets in the embers. The boy lay huddled on the ground watching him.

The new snow lay in skifts all through the woods, along the limbs and cupped in the leaves, all of it already gray with ash. They hiked out to where they'd left the cart and he put the knapsack in and pushed it out to the road. No tracks. They stood listening in the utter silence. Then they set out along the road through the gray slush, the boy at his side with his hands in his pockets.

They trudged all day, the boy in silence. By afternoon the slush had melted off the road and by evening it was dry. They didnt stop. How many miles? Ten, twelve. They used to play quoits in the road with four big steel washers they'd found in a hardware store but these were gone with everything else. That night they camped in a ravine and built a fire against a small stone bluff and ate their last tin of food. He'd put it by because it was the boy's favorite, pork and beans. They watched it bubble slowly in the coals and he retrieved the tin with the pliers and they ate in silence. He rinsed the empty tin with water and gave it to the child to drink and that was that. I should have been more careful, he said.

The boy didnt answer.

You have to talk to me.

Okay.

You wanted to know what the bad guys looked like. Now you know. It may happen again. My job is to take care of you. I was appointed to do that by God. I will kill anyone who touches you. Do you understand?

Yes.

He sat there cowled in the blanket. After a while he looked up. Are we still the good guys? he said.

Yes. We're still the good guys.

And we always will be.

Yes. We always will be.

Okay.

In the morning they came up out of the ravine and took to the road again. He'd carved the boy a flute from a piece of roadside cane and he took it from his coat and gave it to him. The boy took it wordlessly. After a while he fell back and after a while the man could hear him playing. A formless music for the age to come. Or perhaps the last music on earth called up from out of the ashes of its ruin. The man turned and looked back at him. He was lost in concentration. The man thought he seemed some sad and solitary changeling child announcing the arrival of a traveling spectacle in shire and village who does not know that behind him the players have all been carried off by wolves.

. . .

He sat crosslegged in the leaves at the crest of a ridge and glassed the valley below them with the binoculars. The still poured shape of a river. The dark brick stacks of a mill. Slate roofs. An old wooden watertower bound with iron hoops. No smoke, no movement of life. He lowered the glasses and sat watching.

What do you see? the boy said.

Nothing.

He handed the binoculars across. The boy slung the strap over his neck and put them to his eyes and adjusted the wheel. Everything about them so still.

I see smoke, he said.

Where.

Past those buildings.

What buildings?

The boy handed the glasses back and he refocused them. The palest wisp. Yes, he said. I see it.

What should we do, Papa?

I think we should take a look. We just have to be careful. If it's a commune they'll have barricades. But it may just be refugees.

Like us.

Yes. Like us.

What if it's the bad guys?

We'll have to take a risk. We need to find something to eat.

They left the cart in the woods and crossed a railroad track and came down a steep bank through dead black ivy. He carried the pistol in his hand. Stay close, he said. He did. They moved through the streets like sappers. One block at a time. A faint smell of woodsmoke on the air. They waited in a store and watched the street but nothing moved. They went through the trash and rubble. Cabinet drawers pulled out into the floor, paper and bloated cardboard boxes. They found nothing. All the stores were rifled years ago, the glass mostly gone from the windows. Inside it was all but too dark to see. They climbed the ribbed steel stairs of an escalator, the boy holding on to his hand. A few dusty suits hanging on a rack. They looked for shoes but there were none. They shuffled through the trash but there was nothing there of any use to them. When they came back he slipped the suit-coats from their hangers and shook them out and folded them across his arm. Let's go, he said.

. . .

He thought there had to be something overlooked but there wasnt. They kicked through the trash in the aisles of a foodmarket. Old packaging and papers and the eternal ash. He scoured the shelves looking for vitamins. He opened the door of a walk-in cooler but the sour rank smell of the dead washed out of the darkness and he quickly closed it again. They stood in the street. He looked at the gray sky. Faint plume of their breath. The boy was exhausted. He took him by the hand. We have to look some more, he said. We have to keep looking.

The houses at the edge of the town offered little more. They climbed the back steps into a kitchen and began to go through the cabinets. The cabinet doors all standing open. A can of bakingpowder. He stood there looking at it. They went through the drawers of a sideboard in the diningroom. They walked into the livingroom. Scrolls of fallen wallpaper lying in the floor like ancient documents. He left the boy sitting on the stairs holding the coats while he went up.

Everything smelled of damp and rot. In the first bedroom a dried corpse with the covers about its neck. Remnants of rotted hair on the pillow. He took hold of the lower hem of the blanket and towed it off the bed and shook it out and folded it under his arm. He went through the bureaus and the closets. A summer dress on a wire hanger. Nothing. He went back down the stairs. It was getting dark. He took the boy by the hand and they went out the front door to the street.

At the top of the hill he turned and studied the town. Darkness coming fast. Darkness and cold. He put two of the coats over the boy's shoulders, swallowing him up parka and all.

I'm really hungry, Papa.

I know.

Will we be able to find our stuff?

Yes. I know where it is.

What if somebody finds it?

They wont find it.

I hope they dont.

They wont. Come on.

What was that?

I didnt hear anything.

Listen.

I dont hear anything.

They listened. Then in the distance he heard a dog bark. He turned and looked toward the darkening town. It's a dog, he said.

A dog?

Yes.

Where did it come from?

I dont know.

We're not going to kill it, are we Papa?

No. We're not going to kill it.

He looked down at the boy. Shivering in his coats. He bent over and kissed him on his gritty brow. We wont hurt the dog, he said. I promise.

They slept in a parked car beneath an overpass with the suitcoats and the blanket piled over them. In the darkness and the silence he could see bits of light that appeared random on the night grid. The higher floors of the buildings were all dark. You'd have to carry up water. You could be smoked out. What were they eating? God knows. They sat wrapped in the coats looking out the window. Who are they, Papa?

I dont know.

.   .   .

He woke in the night and lay listening. He couldnt remember where he was. The thought made him smile. Where are we? he said.

What is it, Papa?

Nothing. We're okay. Go to sleep.

We're going to be okay, arent we Papa?

Yes. We are.

And nothing bad is going to happen to us.

That's right.

Because we're carrying the fire.

Yes. Because we're carrying the fire.

In the morning a cold rain was falling. It gusted over the car even under the overpass and it danced in the road beyond. They sat and watched through the water on the glass. By the time it had slacked a good part of the day was gone. They left the coats and the blanket in the floor of the back seat and went up the road to search through more of the houses. Woodsmoke on the damp air. They never heard the dog again.

They found some utensils and a few pieces of clothing. A sweatshirt. Some plastic they could use for a tarp. He was sure they were being watched but he saw no one. In a pantry they came upon part of a sack of cornmeal that rats had been at in the long ago. He sifted the meal through a section of windowscreen and collected a small handful of dried turds and they built a fire on the concrete porch of the house and made cakes of the meal and cooked them over a piece of tin. Then they ate them slowly one by one. He wrapped the few remaining in a paper and put them in the knapsack.

The boy was sitting on the steps when he saw something move at the rear of the house across the road. A face was looking at him. A boy, about his age, wrapped in an outsized wool coat with the sleeves turned back. He stood up. He ran across the road and up the drive. No one there. He looked toward the house and then he ran to the bottom of the yard through the dead weeds to a still black creek. Come back, he called. I wont hurt you. He was standing there crying when his father came sprinting across the road and seized him by the arm.

What are you doing? he hissed. What are you doing?

There's a little boy, Papa. There's a little boy.

There's no little boy. What are you doing?

Yes there is. I saw him.

I told you to stay put. Didnt I tell you? Now we've got to go. Come on.

I just wanted to see him, Papa. I just wanted to see him.

The man took him by the arm and they went back up through the yard. The boy would not stop crying and he would not stop looking back. Come on, the man said. We've got to go.

I want to see him, Papa.

There's no one to see. Do you want to die? Is that what you want?

I dont care, the boy said, sobbing. I dont care.

The man stopped. He stopped and squatted and held him. I'm sorry, he said. Dont say that. You musnt say that.

They made their way back through the wet streets to the viaduct and collected the coats and the blanket from the car and went on to the railway embankment where they climbed up and crossed the tracks into the woods and got the cart and headed out to the highway.

What if that little boy doesnt have anybody to take care of him? he said. What if he doesnt have a papa?

There are people there. They were just hiding.

He pushed the cart out into the road and stood there. He could see the tracks of the truck through the wet ash, faint and washed out, but there. He thought that he could smell them. The boy was pulling at his coat. Papa, he said.

What?

I'm afraid for that little boy.

I know. But he'll be all right.

We should go get him, Papa. We could get him and take him with us. We could take him and we could take the dog. The dog could catch something to eat.

We cant.

And I'd give that little boy half of my food.

Stop it. We cant.

He was crying again. What about the little boy? he sobbed. What about the little boy?

At a crossroads they sat in the dusk and he spread out the pieces of the map in the road and studied them. He put his finger down. This is us, he said. Right here. The boy wouldnt look. He sat studying the twisted matrix of routes in red and black with his finger at the junction where he thought that they might be. As if he'd see their small selves crouching there. We could go back, the boy said softly. It's not so far. It's not too late.

They made a dry camp in a woodlot not far from the road. They could find no sheltered place to make a fire that would not be seen so they made none. They ate each of them two of the cornmeal cakes and they slept together huddled on the ground in the coats and blankets. He held the child and after a while the child stopped shivering and after a while he slept.

The dog that he remembers followed us for two days. I tried to coax it to come but it would not. I made a noose of wire to catch it. There were three cartridges in the pistol. None to spare. She walked away down the road. The boy looked after her and then he looked at me and then he looked at the dog and he began to cry and to beg for the dog's life and I promised I would not hurt the dog. A trellis of a dog with the hide stretched over it. The next day it was gone. That is the dog he remembers. He doesnt remember any little boys.

. . .

He'd put a handful of dried raisins in a cloth in his pocket and at noon they sat in the dead grass by the side of the road and ate them. The boy looked at him. That's all there is, isnt it? he said.

Yes.

Are we going to die now?

No.

What are we going to do?

We're going to drink some water. Then we're going to keep going down the road.

Okay.

In the evening they tramped out across a field trying to find a place where their fire would not be seen. Dragging the cart behind them over the ground. So little of promise in that country. Tomorrow they would find something to eat. Night overtook them on a muddy road. They crossed into a field and plodded on toward a distant stand of trees skylighted stark and black against the last of the visible world. By the time they got there it was dark of night. He held the boy's hand and kicked up limbs and brush and got a fire going. The wood was damp but he shaved the dead bark off with his knife and he stacked brush and sticks all about to dry in the heat. Then he spread the sheet of plastic on the ground and got the coats and blankets from the cart and he took off their damp and muddy shoes and they sat there in silence with their hands out-held to the flames. He tried to think of something to say but he could not. He'd had this feeling before, beyond the numbness and the dull despair. The world shrinking down about a raw core of parsible entities. The names of things slowly following those things into oblivion. Colors. The names of birds. Things to eat. Finally the names of things one believed to be true. More fragile than he would have thought. How much was gone already? The sacred idiom shorn of its referents and so of its reality. Drawing down like something trying to preserve heat. In time to wink out forever.

They slept through the night in their exhaustion and in the morning the fire was dead and black on the ground. He pulled on his muddy shoes and went to gather wood, blowing on his cupped hands. So cold. It could be November. It could be later. He got a fire going and walked out to the edge of the woodlot and stood looking over the countryside. The dead fields. A barn in the distance.

They hiked out along the dirt road and along a hill where a house had once stood. It had burned long ago. The rusted shape of a furnace standing in the black water of the cellar. Sheets of charred metal roofing crumpled in the fields where the wind had blown it. In the barn they scavenged a few handfuls of some grain he did not recognize out of the dusty floor of a metal hopper and stood eating it dust and all. Then they set out across the fields toward the road.

They followed a stone wall past the remains of an orchard. The trees in their ordered rows gnarled and black and the fallen limbs thick on the ground. He stopped and looked across the fields. Wind in the east. The soft ash moving in the furrows. Stopping. Moving again. He'd seen it all before. Shapes of dried blood in the stubble grass and gray coils of viscera where the slain had been field-dressed and hauled away. The wall beyond held a frieze of human heads, all faced alike, dried and caved with their taut grins and shrunken eyes. They wore gold rings in their leather ears and in the wind their sparse and ratty hair twisted about on their skulls. The teeth in their sockets like dental molds, the crude tattoos etched in some homebrewed woad faded in the beggared sunlight. Spiders, swords, targets. A dragon. Runic slogans, creeds misspelled. Old scars with old motifs stitched along their borders. The heads not truncheoned shapeless had been flayed of their skins and the raw skulls painted and signed across the forehead in a scrawl and one white bone skull had the plate sutures etched carefully in ink like a blueprint for assembly. He looked back at the boy. Standing by the cart in the wind. He looked at the dry grass where it moved and at the dark and twisted trees in their rows. A few shreds of clothing blown against the wall, everything gray in the ash. He walked along the wall passing the masks in a last review and through a stile and on to where the boy was waiting. He put his arm around his shoulder. Okay, he said. Let's go.

He'd come to see a message in each such late history, a message and a warning, and so this tableau of the slain and the devoured did prove to be. He woke in the morning and turned over in the blanket and looked back down the road through the trees the way they'd come in time to see the marchers appear four abreast. Dressed in clothing of every description, all wearing red scarves at their necks. Red or orange, as close to red as they could find. He put his hand on the boy's head. Shh, he said.

What is it, Papa?

People on the road. Keep your face down. Dont look.

No smoke from the dead fire. Nothing to be seen of the cart. He wallowed into the ground and lay watching across his forearm. An army in tennis shoes, tramping. Carrying three-foot lengths of pipe with leather wrappings. Lanyards at the wrist. Some of the pipes were threaded through with lengths of chain fitted at their ends with every manner of bludgeon. They clanked past, marching with a swaying gait like wind-up toys. Bearded, their breath smoking through their masks. Shh, he said. Shh. The phalanx following carried spears or lances tasseled with ribbons, the long blades hammered out of trucksprings in some crude forge upcountry. The boy lay with his face in his arms, terrified. They passed two hundred feet away, the ground shuddering lightly. Tramping. Behind them came wagons drawn by slaves in harness and piled with goods of war and after that the women, perhaps a dozen in number, some of them pregnant, and lastly a supplementary consort of catamites illclothed against the cold and fitted in dogcollars and yoked each to each. All passed on. They lay listening.

Are they gone, Papa?

Yes, they're gone.

Did you see them?

Yes.

Were they the bad guys?

Yes, they were the bad guys.

There's a lot of them, those bad guys.

Yes there are. But they're gone.

They stood and brushed themselves off, listening to the silence in the distance.

Where are they going, Papa?

I dont know. They're on the move. It's not a good sign.

Why isnt it a good sign?

It just isnt. We need to get the map and take a look.

They pulled the cart from the brush with which they'd covered it and he raised it up and piled the blankets in and the coats and they pushed on out to the road and stood looking where the last of that ragged horde seemed to hang like an afterimage in the disturbed air.

. . .

In the afternoon it started to snow again. They stood watching the pale gray flakes sift down out of the sullen murk. They trudged on. A frail slush forming over the dark surface of the road. The boy kept falling behind and he stopped and waited for him. Stay with me, he said.

You walk too fast.

I'll go slower.

They went on.

You're not talking again.

I'm talking.

You want to stop?

I always want to stop.

We have to be more careful. I have to be more careful.

I know.

We'll stop. Okay?

Okay.

We just have to find a place.

Okay.

The falling snow curtained them about. There was no way to see anything at either side of the road. He was coughing again and the boy was shivering, the two of them side by side under the sheet of plastic, pushing the grocery cart through the snow. Finally he stopped. The boy was shaking uncontrollably.

We have to stop, he said.

It's really cold.

I know.

Where are we?

Where are we?

Yes.

I dont know.

If we were going to die would you tell me?

I dont know. We're not going to die.

They left the cart overturned in a field of sedge and he took the coats and the blankets wrapped in the plastic tarp and they set out. Hold on to my coat, he said. Dont let go. They crossed through the sedge to a fence and climbed through, holding down the wire for each other with their hands. The wire was cold and it creaked in the staples. It was darkening fast. They went on. What they came to was a cedar wood, the trees dead and black but still full enough to hold the snow. Beneath each one a precious circle of dark earth and cedar duff.

. . .

They settled under a tree and piled the blankets and coats on the ground and he wrapped the boy in one of the blankets and set to raking up the dead needles in a pile. He kicked a cleared place in the snow out where the fire wouldnt set the tree alight and he carried wood from the other trees, breaking off the limbs and shaking away the snow. When he struck the lighter to the rich tinder the fire crackled instantly and he knew that it would not last long. He looked at the boy. I've got to go for more wood, he said. I'll be in the neighborhood. Okay?

Where's the neighborhood?

It just means I wont be far.

Okay.

The snow by now was half a foot on the ground. He floundered out through the trees pulling up the fallen branches where they stuck out of the snow and by the time he had an armload and made his way back to the fire it had burned down to a nest of quaking embers. He threw the branches on the fire and set out again. Hard to stay ahead. The woods were getting dark and the firelight did not reach far. If he hurried he only grew faint. When he looked behind him the boy was trudging through snow half way to his knees gathering limbs and piling them in his arms.

The snow fell nor did it cease to fall. He woke all night and got up and coaxed the fire to life again. He'd unfolded the tarp and propped one end of it up beneath the tree to try and reflect back the heat from the fire. He looked at the boy's face sleeping in the orange light. The sunken cheeks streaked with black. He fought back the rage. Useless. He didnt think the boy could travel much more. Even if it stopped snowing the road would be all but impassable. The snow whispered down in the stillness and the sparks rose and dimmed and died in the eternal blackness.

He was half asleep when he heard a crashing in the woods. Then another. He sat up. The fire was down to scattered flames among the embers. He listened. The long dry crack of shearing limbs. Then another crash. He reached and shook the boy. Wake up, he said. We have to go.

He rubbed the sleep from his eyes with the backs of his hands. What is it? he said. What is it, Papa?

Come on. We have to move.

What is it?

It's the trees. They're falling down.

The boy sat up and looked about wildly.

It's all right, the man said. Come on. We need to hurry.

He scooped up the bedding and he folded it and wrapped the tarp around it. He looked up. The snow drifted into his eyes. The fire was little more than coals and it gave no light and the wood was nearly gone and the trees were falling all about them in the blackness. The boy clung to him. They moved away and he tried to find a clear space in the darkness but finally he put down the tarp and they just sat and pulled the blankets over them and he held the boy against him. The whump of the falling trees and the low boom of the loads of snow exploding on the ground set the woods to shuddering. He held the boy and told him it would be all right and that it would stop soon and after a while it did. The dull bedlam dying in the distance. And again, solitary and far away. Then nothing. There, he said. I think that's it. He dug a tunnel under one of the fallen trees, scooping away the snow with his arms, his frozen hands clawed inside his sleeves. They dragged in their bedding and the tarp and after a while they slept again for all the bitter cold.

When day broke he pushed his way out of their den, the tarp heavy with snow. He stood and looked about. It had stopped snowing and the cedar trees lay about in hillocks of snow and broken limbs and a few standing trunks that stood stripped and burntlooking in that graying landscape. He trudged out through the drifts leaving the boy to sleep under the tree like some hibernating animal. The snow was almost to his knees. In the field the dead sedge was drifted nearly out of sight and the snow stood in razor kerfs atop the fencewires and the silence was breathless. He stood leaning on a post coughing. He'd little idea where the cart was and he thought that he was getting stupid and that his head wasnt working right. Concentrate, he said. You have to think. When he turned to go back the boy was calling him.

We have to go, he said. We cant stay here.
The boy stared bleakly at the gray drifts.
Come on.

They made their way out to the fence.

Where are we going? the boy said.

We have to find the cart.

He just stood there, his hands in the armpits of his parka.

Come on, the man said. You have to come on.

He waded out across the drifted fields. The snow lay deep and gray. Already there was a fresh fall of ash on it. He struggled on a few more feet and then turned and looked back. The boy had fallen. He dropped the armload of blankets and the tarp and went back and picked him up. He was already shivering. He picked him up and held him. I'm sorry, he said. I'm sorry.

They were a long time finding the cart. He pulled it upright out of the drifts and dug out the knapsack and shook it out and opened it and stuffed in one of the blankets. He put the pack and the other blankets and the coats in the basket and picked up the boy and set him on top and unlaced his shoes and pulled them off. Then he got out his knife and set about cutting up one of the coats and wrapping the boy's feet. He used the entire coat and then he cut big squares of plastic out of the tarp and gathered them up from underneath and wrapped and tied them at the boy's ankles with the lining from the coatsleeves. He stood back. The boy looked down. Now you, Papa, he said. He wrapped one of the coats around the boy and then he sat on the tarp in the snow and wrapped his own feet. He stood and warmed his hands inside his parka and then packed their shoes into the knapsack along with the binoculars and the boy's truck. He shook out the tarp and folded it and tied it with the other blankets on top of the pack and shouldered it up and then took a last look through the basket but that was it. Let's go, he said. The boy took one last look back at the cart and then followed him out to the road.

It was harder going even than he would have guessed. In an hour they'd made perhaps a mile. He stopped and looked back at the boy. The boy stopped and waited.

You think we're going to die, dont you?

I dont know.

We're not going to die.

Okay.

But you dont believe me.

I dont know.

Why do you think we're going to die?

I dont know.

Stop saying I dont know.

Okay.

Why do you think we're going to die?

We dont have anything to eat.

We'll find something.

Okay.

How long do you think people can go without food?

I dont know.

But how long do you think?

Maybe a few days.

And then what? You fall over dead?

Yes.

Well you dont. It takes a long time. We have water. That's the most important thing. You dont last very long without water.

Okay.

But you dont believe me.

I dont know.

He studied him. Standing there with his hands in the pockets of the outsized pinstriped suitcoat.

Do you think I lie to you?

No.

But you think I might lie to you about dying.

Yes.

Okay. I might. But we're not dying.

Okay.

He studied the sky. There were days when the ashen overcast thinned and now the standing trees along the road made the faintest of shadows over the snow. They went on. The boy wasnt doing well. He stopped and checked his feet and retied the plastic. When the snow started to melt it was going to be hard to keep their feet dry. They stopped often to rest. He'd no strength to carry the child. They sat on the pack and ate handfuls of the dirty snow. By afternoon it was beginning to melt. They passed a burned house, just the brick chimney standing in the yard. They were on the road all day, such day as there was. Such few hours. They might have covered three miles.

He thought the road would be so bad that no one would be on it but he was wrong. They camped almost in the road itself and built a great fire, dragging dead limbs out of the snow and piling them on the flames to hiss and steam. There was no help for it. The few blankets they had would not keep them warm. He tried to stay awake. He would jerk upright out of his sleep and slap about him looking for the pistol. The boy was so thin. He watched him while he slept. Taut face and hollow eyes. A strange beauty. He got up and dragged more wood onto the fire.

They walked out to the road and stood. There were tracks in the snow. A wagon. Some sort of wheeled vehicle. Something with rubber tires by the narrow treadmarks. Bootprints between the wheels. Someone had passed in the dark going south. In the early dawn at latest. Running the road in the night. He stood thinking about that. He walked the tracks carefully. They'd passed within fifty feet of the fire and had not even slowed to look. He stood looking back up the road. The boy watched him.

We need to get out of the road.

Why, Papa?

Someone's coming.

Is it bad guys?

Yes. I'm afraid so.

They could be good guys. Couldnt they?

He didnt answer. He looked at the sky out of old habit but there was nothing to see.

What are we going to do, Papa?

Let's go.

Can we go back to the fire?

No. Come on. We probably dont have much time.

I'm really hungry.

I know.

What are we going to do?

We have to hole up. Get off the road.

Will they see our tracks?

Yes.

What can we do about it?

I dont know.

Will they know what we are?

What?

If they see our tracks. Will they know what we are?

He looked back at their great round tracks in the snow.

They'll figure it out, he said.

Then he stopped.

We need to think about this. Let's go back to the fire.

He'd thought to find some place in the road where the snow had melted off completely but then he thought that since their tracks would not reappear on the far side it would be no help. They kicked snow over the fire and went on through the trees and circled and came back. They hurried, leaving a maze of tracks and then they set out back north through the woods keeping the road in view.

The site they picked was simply the highest ground they came to and it gave views north along the road and over-looked their backtrack. He spread the tarp in the wet snow and wrapped the boy in the blankets. You're going to be cold, he said. But maybe we wont be here long. Within the hour two men came down the road almost at a lope. When they had passed he stood up to watch them. And when he did they stopped and one of them looked back. He froze. He was wrapped in one of the gray blankets and he would have been hard to see but not impossible. But he thought probably they had smelled the smoke. They stood talking. Then they went on. He sat down. It's okay, he said. We just have to wait. But I think its okay.

. . .

They'd had no food and little sleep in five days and in this condition on the outskirts of a small town they came upon a once grand house sited on a rise above the road. The boy stood holding his hand. The snow was largely melted on the macadam and in the southfacing fields and woods. They stood there. The plastic bags over their feet had long since worn through and their feet were wet and cold. The house was tall and stately with white doric columns across the front. A port cochere at the side. A gravel drive that curved up through a field of dead grass. The windows were oddly intact.

What is this place, Papa?

Shh. Let's just stand here and listen.

There was nothing. The wind rustling the dead roadside bracken. A distant creaking. Door or shutter.

I think we should take a look.

Papa let's not go up there.

It's okay.

I dont think we should go up there.

It's okay. We have to take a look.

They approached slowly up the drive. No tracks in the random patches of melting snow. A tall hedge of dead privet. An ancient birdsnest lodged in the dark wicker of it. They stood in the yard studying the facade. The handmade brick of the house kilned out of the dirt it stood on. The peeling paint hanging in long dry sleavings down the columns and from the buckled soffits. A lamp that hung from a long chain overhead. The boy clung to him as they climbed the steps. One of the windows was slightly open and a cord ran from it and across the porch to vanish in the grass. He held the boy's hand and they crossed the porch. Chattel slaves had once trod those boards bearing food and drink on silver trays. They went to the window and looked in.

What if there's someone here, Papa?

There's no one here.

We should go, Papa.

We've got to find something to eat. We have no choice.

We could find something somewhere else.

It's going to be all right. Come on.

He took the pistol from his belt and tried the door. It swung slowly in on its great brass hinges. They stood listening. Then they stepped into a broad foyer floored in a domino of black and white marble tiles. A broad staircase ascending. Fine Morris paper on the walls, waterstained and sagging. The plaster ceiling was bellied in great swags and the yellowed dentil molding was bowed and sprung from the upper walls. To the left through the doorway stood a large walnut buffet in what must have been the diningroom. The doors and the drawers were gone but the rest of it was too large to burn. They stood in the doorway. Piled in a windrow in one corner of the room was a great heap of clothing. Clothes and shoes. Belts. Coats. Blankets and old sleeping bags. He would have ample time later to think about that. The boy hung on to his hand. He was terrified. They crossed the foyer to the room on the far side and walked in and stood. A great hall of a room with ceilings twice the height of the doors. A fireplace with raw brick showing where the wooden mantel and surround had been pried away and burned. There were mattresses and bedding arranged on the floor in front of the hearth. Papa, the boy whispered. Shh, he said.

The ashes were cold. Some blackened pots stood about. He squatted on his heels and picked one up and smelled it and put it back. He stood and looked out the window. Gray trampled grass. Gray snow. The cord that came through the window was tied to a brass bell and the bell was fixed in a rough wooden jig that had been nailed to the window molding. He held the boy's hand and they went down a narrow back hallway into the kitchen. Trash piled everywhere. A ruststained sink. Smell of mold and excrement. They went on into the adjoining small room, perhaps a pantry.

In the floor of this room was a door or hatch and it was locked with a large padlock made of stacked steel plates. He stood looking at it.

Papa, the boy said. We should go. Papa.

There's a reason this is locked.

The boy pulled at his hand. He was almost in tears. Papa? he said.

We've got to eat.

I'm not hungry, Papa. I'm not.

We need to find a prybar or something.

They pushed out through the back door, the boy hanging on to him. He shoved the pistol in his belt and stood looking out over the yard. There was a brick walkway and the twisted and wiry shape of what once had been a row of boxwoods. In the yard was an old iron harrow propped up on piers of stacked brick and someone had wedged between the rails of it a forty gallon castiron cauldron of the kind once used for rendering hogs. Underneath were the ashes of a fire and blackened billets of wood. Off to one side a small wagon with rubber tires. All these things he saw and did not see. At the far side of the yard was an old wooden smokehouse and a toolshed. He crossed half dragging the child and went sorting through tools standing in a barrel under the shed roof. He came up with a longhandled spade and hefted it in his hand. Come on, he said.

Back in the house he chopped at the wood around the haspstaple and finally jammed the blade under the staple and pried it up. It was bolted through the wood and the whole thing came up lock and all. He kicked the blade of the shovel under the edge of the boards and stopped and got his lighter out. Then he stood on the tang of the shovel and raised the edge of the hatch and leaned and got hold of it. Papa, the boy whispered.

He stopped. Listen to me, he said. Just stop it. We're

starving. Do you understand? Then he raised the hatch door and swung it over and let it down on the floor behind.

Just wait here, he said.

I'm going with you.

I thought you were scared.

I am scared.

Okay. Just stay close behind me.

He started down the rough wooden steps. He ducked his head and then flicked the lighter and swung the flame out over the darkness like an offering. Coldness and damp. An ungodly stench. The boy clutched at his coat. He could see part of a stone wall. Clay floor. An old mattress darkly stained. He crouched and stepped down again and held out the light. Huddled against the back wall were naked people, male and female, all trying to hide, shielding their faces with their hands. On the mattress lay a man with his legs gone to the hip and the stumps of them blackened and burnt. The smell was hideous.

Jesus, he whispered.

Then one by one they turned and blinked in the pitiful light. Help us, they whispered. Please help us.

Christ, he said. Oh Christ.

He turned and grabbed the boy. Hurry, he said. Hurry.

He'd dropped the lighter. No time to look. He pushed the boy up the stairs. Help us, they called.

Hurry.

A bearded face appeared blinking at the foot of the stairs. Please, he called. Please.

Hurry. For God's sake hurry.

He shoved the boy through the hatch and sent him sprawling. He stood and got hold of the door and swung it over and let it slam down and he turned to grab the boy but the boy had gotten up and was doing his little dance of terror. For the love of God will you come on, he hissed. But the boy was pointing out the window and when he looked he went cold all over. Coming across the field toward the house were four bearded men and two women. He grabbed the boy by the hand. Christ, he said. Run. Run.

They tore through the house to the front door and down the steps. Half way down the drive he dragged the boy into the field. He looked back. They were partly screened by the ruins of the privet but he knew they had minutes at most and maybe no minutes at all. At the bottom of the field they crashed through a stand of dead cane and out into the road and crossed into the woods on the far side. He redoubled his grip on the boy's wrist. Run, he whispered. We have to run. He looked toward the house but he could see nothing. If they came down the drive they would see him running through the trees with the boy. This is the moment. This is the moment. He fell to the ground and pulled the boy to him. Shh, he said. Shh.

Are they going to kill us? Papa?

Shh.

They lay in the leaves and the ash with their hearts pounding. He was going to start coughing. He'd have put his hand over his mouth but the boy was holding on to it and would not let go and in the other hand he was holding the pistol. He had to concentrate to stifle the cough and at the same time he was trying to listen. He swung his chin through the leaves, trying to see. Keep your head down, he whispered.

Are they coming?

No.

They crawled slowly through the leaves toward what looked like lower ground. He lay listening, holding the boy. He could hear them in the road talking. Voice of a woman. Then he heard them in the dry leaves. He took the boy's hand and pushed the revolver into it. Take it, he whispered. Take it. The boy was terrified. He put his arm around him and held him. His body so thin. Dont be afraid, he said. If they find you you are going to have to do it. Do you understand? Shh. No crying. Do you hear me? You know how to do it. You put it in your mouth and point it up. Do it quick and hard. Do you understand? Stop crying. Do you understand?

I think so.

No. Do you understand?

Yes.

Say yes I do Papa.

Yes I do Papa.

He looked down at him. All he saw was terror. He took the gun from him. No you dont, he said.

I dont know what to do, Papa. I dont know what to do. Where will you be?

It's okay.

I dont know what to do.

Shh. I'm right here. I wont leave you.

You promise.

Yes. I promise. I was going to run. To try and lead them away. But I cant leave you.

Papa?

Shh. Stay down.

I'm so scared.

Shh.

They lay listening. Can you do it? When the time comes? When the time comes there will be no time. Now is the time. Curse God and die. What if it doesnt fire? It has to fire. What if it doesnt fire? Could you crush that beloved skull with a rock? Is there such a being within you of which you know nothing? Can there be? Hold him in your arms. Just so. The soul is quick. Pull him toward you. Kiss him. Quickly.

He waited. The small nickelplated revolver in his hand. He was going to cough. He put his whole mind to holding it back. He tried to listen but he could hear nothing. I wont leave you, he whispered. I wont ever leave you. Do you understand? He lay in the leaves holding the trembling child. Clutching the revolver. All through the long dusk and into the dark. Cold and starless. Blessed. He began to believe they had a chance. We just have to wait, he whispered. So cold. He tried to think but his mind swam. He was so weak. All his talk about running. He couldnt run. When it was truly black about them he unfastened the straps on the backpack and pulled out the blankets and spread them over the boy and soon the boy was sleeping.

In the night he heard hideous shrieks coming from the house and he tried to put his hands over the boy's ears and after a while the screaming stopped. He lay listening. Coming through the canebrake into the road he'd seen a box. A thing like a child's playhouse. He realized it was where they lay watching the road. Lying in wait and ringing the bell in the house for their companions to come. He dozed and woke. What is coming? Footsteps in the leaves. No. Just the wind. Nothing. He sat up and looked toward the house but he could see only darkness. He shook the boy awake. Come on, he said. We have to go. The boy didnt answer but he knew he was awake. He pulled the blankets free and strapped them onto the knapsack. Come on, he whispered.

. . .

They set out through the dark woods. There was a moon somewhere beyond the ashen overcast and they could just make out the trees. They staggered on like drunks. If they find us they'll kill us, wont they Papa.

Shh. No more talking.

Wont they Papa.

Shh. Yes. Yes they will.

He'd no idea what direction they might have taken and his fear was that they might circle and return to the house. He tried to remember if he knew anything about that or if it were only a fable. In what direction did lost men veer? Perhaps it changed with hemispheres. Or handedness. Finally he put it out of his mind. The notion that there could be anything to correct for. His mind was betraying him. Phantoms not heard from in a thousand years rousing slowly from their sleep. Correct for that. The boy was tottering on his feet. He asked to be carried, stumbling and slurring his words, and the man did carry him and he fell asleep on his shoulder instantly. He knew he couldnt carry him far.

. . .

He woke in the dark of the woods in the leaves shivering violently. He sat up and felt about for the boy. He held his hand to the thin ribs. Warmth and movement. Heartbeat.

When he woke again it was almost light enough to see. He threw back the blanket and stood and almost fell. He steadied himself and tried to see about him in the gray woods. How far had they come? He walked to the top of a rise and crouched and watched the day accrue. The chary dawn, the cold illucid world. In the distance what looked to be a pine wood, raw and black. A colorless world of wire and crepe. He went back and got the boy and made him sit up. His head kept slumping forward. We have to go, he said. We have to go.

He carried him across the field, stopping to rest each fifty counted steps. When he got to the pines he knelt and laid him in the gritty duff and covered him with the blankets and sat watching him. He looked like something out of a deathcamp. Starved, exhausted, sick with fear. He leaned and kissed him and got up and walked out to the edge of the woods and then he walked the perimeter round to see if they were safe.

Across the fields to the south he could see the shape of a house and a barn. Beyond the trees the curve of a road. A long drive with dead grass. Dead ivy along a stone wall and a mailbox and a fence along the road and the dead trees beyond. Cold and silent. Shrouded in the carbon fog. He walked back and sat beside the boy. It was desperation that had led him to such carelessness and he knew that he could not do that again. No matter what.

The boy wouldnt wake for hours. Still if he did he'd be terrified. It had happened before. He thought about waking him but he knew that he wouldnt remember anything if he did. He'd trained him to lie in the woods like a fawn. For how long? In the end he took the pistol from his belt and laid it alongside him under the blankets and rose and set out.

He came upon the barn from the hill above it, stopping to watch and to listen. He made his way down through the ruins of an old apple orchard, black and gnarly stumps, dead grass to his knees. He stood in the door of the barn and listened. Pale slatted light. He walked along the dusty stalls. He stood in the center of the barn bay and listened but there was nothing. He climbed the ladder to the loft and he was so weak he wasnt sure he was going to make it to the top. He walked down to the end of the loft and looked out the high gable window at the country below, the pieced land dead and gray, the fence, the road.

There were bales of hay in the loft floor and he squatted and sorted a handful of seeds from them and sat chewing. Coarse and dry and dusty. They had to contain some nutrition. He rose and rolled two of the bales across the floor and let them fall into the bay below. Two dusty thumps. He went back to the gable and stood studying what he could see of the house beyond the corner of the barn. Then he climbed back down the ladder.

The grass between the house and the barn looked untrodden. He crossed to the porch. The porch screening rotted and falling away. A child's bicycle. The kitchen door stood open and he crossed the porch and stood in the doorway. Cheap plywood paneling curled with damp. Collapsing into the room. A red formica table. He crossed the room and opened the refrigerator door. Something sat on one of the racks in a coat of gray fur. He shut the door. Trash everywhere. He took a broom from the corner and poked about with the handle. He climbed onto the counter and felt his way through the dust on top of the cabinets. A mousetrap. A packet of something. He blew away the dust. It was a grape flavored powder to make drinks with. He put it in the pocket of his coat.

He went through the house room by room. He found nothing. A spoon in a bedside drawer. He put that in his pocket. He thought there might be some clothes in a closet or some bedding but there wasnt. He went back out and crossed to the garage. He sorted through tools. Rakes. A shovel. Jars of nails and bolts on a shelf. A boxcutter. He held it to the light and looked at the rusty blade and put it back. Then he picked it up again. He took a screwdriver from a coffee can and opened the handle. Inside were four new blades. He took out the old blade and laid it on the shelf and put in one of the new ones and screwed the handle back together and retracted the blade and put the cutter in his pocket. Then he picked up the screwdriver and put that in his pocket as well.

He walked back out to the barn. He had a piece of cloth that he intended to use to collect seeds from the haybales but when he got to the barn he stopped and stood listening to the wind. A creaking of tin somewhere high in the roof above him. There was yet a lingering odor of cows in the barn and he stood there thinking about cows and he realized they were extinct. Was that true? There could be a cow somewhere being fed and cared for. Could there? Fed what? Saved for what? Beyond the open door the dead grass rasped dryly in the wind. He walked out and stood looking across the fields toward the pine wood where the boy lay sleeping. He walked up through the orchard and then he stopped again. He'd stepped on something. He took a step back and knelt and parted the grass with his hands. It was an apple. He picked it up and held it to the light. Hard and brown and shriveled. He wiped it with the cloth and bit into it. Dry and almost tasteless. But an apple. He ate it entire, seeds and all. He held the stem between his thumb and forefinger and let it drop. Then he went treading softly through the grass. His feet were still wrapped in the remnants of the coat and the shreds of tarp and he sat and untied them and stuffed the wrappings in his pocket and went down the rows barefoot. By the time he got to the bottom of the orchard he had four more apples and he put them in his pocket and came back. He went row by row till he'd trod a puzzle in the grass. He'd more apples than he could carry. He felt out the spaces about the trunks and filled his pockets full and he piled apples in the hood of his parka behind his head and carried apples stacked along his forearm against his chest. He dumped them in a pile at the door of the barn and sat there and wrapped up his numb feet.

In the mudroom off the kitchen he'd seen an old wicker basket full of masonjars. He dragged the basket out into the floor and set the jars out of it and then tipped over the basket and tapped out the dirt. Then he stopped. What had he seen? A drainpipe. A trellis. The dark serpentine of a dead vine running down it like the track of some enterprise upon a graph. He stood up and walked back through the kitchen and out into the yard and stood looking at the house. The windows giving back the gray and nameless day. The drainpipe ran down the corner of the porch. He was still holding the basket and he set it down in the grass and climbed the steps again. The pipe came down the corner post and into a concrete tank. He brushed away the trash and rotted bits of screening from the cover. He went back into the kitchen and got the broom and came out and swept the cover clean and set the broom in the corner and lifted the cover from the tank. Inside was a tray filled with a wet gray sludge from the roof mixed with a compost of dead leaves and twigs. He lifted out the tray and set it in the floor. Underneath was white gravel. He scooped back the gravel with his hand. The tank beneath was filled with charcoal, pieces burned out of whole sticks and limbs in carbon effigies of the trees themselves. He put the tray back. In the floor was a green brass ringpull. He reached and got the broom and swept away the ash. There were sawlines in the boards. He swept the boards clean and knelt and hooked his fingers in the ring and lifted the trap door and swung it open. Down there in the darkness was a cistern filled with water so sweet that he could smell it. He lay in the floor on his stomach and reached down. He could just touch the water. He scooted forward and reached again and laved up a handful of it and smelled and tasted it and then drank. He lay there a long time, lifting up the water to his mouth a palmful at a time. Nothing in his memory anywhere of anything so good.

He went back to the mudroom and returned with two of the jars and an old blue enameled pan. He wiped out the pan and dipped it full of water and used it to clean the jars. Then he reached down and sank one of the jars till it was full and raised it up dripping. The water was so clear. He held it to the light. A single bit of sediment coiling in the jar on some slow hydraulic axis. He tipped the jar and drank and he drank slowly but still he drank nearly the whole jar. He sat there with his stomach bloated. He could have drunk more but he didnt. He poured the remaining water into the other jar and rinsed it out and he filled both jars and then let down the wooden cover over the cistern and rose and with his pockets full of apples and carrying the jars of water he set out across the fields toward the pine wood.

He was gone longer than he'd meant to be and he hurried his steps the best he could, the water swinging and gurgling in the shrunken swag of his gut. He stopped to rest and began again. When he got to the woods the boy did not look as if he'd even stirred and he knelt and set the jars carefully in the duff and picked up the pistol and put it in his belt and then he just sat there watching him.

They spent the afternoon sitting wrapped in the blankets and eating apples. Sipping the water from the jars. He took the packet of grape flavor from his pocket and opened it and poured it into the jar and stirred it and gave it to the boy. You did good Papa, he said. He slept while the boy kept watch and in the evening they got out their shoes and put them on and went down to the farmhouse and collected the rest of the apples. They filled three jars with water and screwed on the two-piece caps from a box of them he'd found on a shelf in the mudroom. Then he wrapped everything in one of the blankets and packed it into the knapsack and tied the other blankets across the top of the knapsack and shouldered it up. They stood in the door watching the light draw down over the world to the west. Then they went down the drive and set out upon the road again.

.   .   .

The boy hung on to his coat and he kept to the edge of the road and tried to feel out the pavement under his feet in the dark. In the distance he could hear thunder and after a while there were dim shudderings of light ahead of them. He got out the plastic sheeting from the knapsack but there was hardly enough of it left to cover them and after a while it began to rain. They stumbled along side by side. There was nowhere to go. They had the hoods of their coats up but the coats were getting wet and heavy from the rain. He stopped in the road and tried to rearrange the tarp. The boy was shaking badly.

You're freezing, arent you?

Yes.

If we stop we'll get really cold.

I'm really cold now.

What do you want to do?

Can we stop?

Yes. Okay. We can stop.

It was as long a night as he could remember out of a great plenty of such nights. They lay on the wet ground by the side of the road under the blankets with the rain rattling on the tarp and he held the boy and after a while the boy stopped shaking and after a while he slept. The thunder trundled away to the north and ceased and there was just the rain. He slept and woke and the rain slackened and after a while it stopped. He wondered if it was even midnight. He was coughing and it got worse and it woke the child. The dawn was a long time coming. He raised up from time to time to look to the east and after a while it was day.

He wrapped their coats each in turn around the trunk of a small tree and twisted out the water. He had the boy take off his clothes and he wrapped him in one of the blankets and while he stood shivering he wrung the water out of his clothes and passed them back. The ground where they'd slept was dry and they sat there with the blankets draped over them and ate apples and drank water. Then they set out upon the road again, slumped and cowled and shivering in their rags like mendicant friars sent forth to find their keep.

By evening they at least were dry. They studied the pieces of map but he'd little notion of where they were. He stood at a rise in the road and tried to take his bearings in the twilight. They left the pike and took a narrow road through the country and came at last upon a bridge and a dry creek and they crawled down the bank and huddled underneath.

Can we have a fire? the boy said.

We dont have a lighter.

The boy looked away.

I'm sorry. I dropped it. I didnt want to tell you.

That's okay.

I'll find us some flint. I've been looking. And we've still got the little bottle of gasoline.

Okay.

Are you very cold?

I'm okay.

The boy lay with his head in the man's lap. After a while he said: They're going to kill those people, arent they?

Yes.

Why do they have to do that?

I dont know.

Are they going to eat them?

I dont know.

They're going to eat them, arent they?

Yes.

And we couldnt help them because then they'd eat us too.

Yes.

And that's why we couldnt help them.

Yes.

Okay.

They passed through towns that warned people away with messages scrawled on the billboards. The billboards had been whited out with thin coats of paint in order to write on them and through the paint could be seen a pale palimpsest of advertisements for goods which no longer existed. They sat by the side of the road and ate the last of the apples.

What is it? the man said.

Nothing.

We'll find something to eat. We always do.

The boy didnt answer. The man watched him.

That's not it, is it?

It's okay.

Tell me.

The boy looked away down the road.

I want you to tell me. It's okay.

He shook his head.

Look at me, the man said.

He turned and looked. He looked like he'd been crying.

Just tell me.

We wouldnt ever eat anybody, would we?

No. Of course not.

Even if we were starving?

We're starving now.

You said we werent.

I said we werent dying. I didnt say we werent starving.

But we wouldnt.

No. We wouldnt.

No matter what.

No. No matter what.

Because we're the good guys.

Yes.

And we're carrying the fire.

And we're carrying the fire. Yes.

Okay.

He found pieces of flint or chert in a ditch but in the end it was easier to rake the pliers down the side of a rock at the bottom of which he'd made a small pile of tinder soaked in gas. Two more days. Then three. They were starving right enough. The country was looted, ransacked, ravaged. Rifled of every crumb. The nights were blinding cold and casket black and the long reach of the morning had a terrible silence to it. Like a dawn before battle. The boy's candlecolored skin was all but translucent. With his great staring eyes he'd the look of an alien.

He was beginning to think that death was finally upon them and that they should find some place to hide where they would not be found. There were times when he sat watching the boy sleep that he would begin to sob uncontrollably but it wasnt about death. He wasnt sure what it was about but he thought it was about beauty or about goodness. Things that he'd no longer any way to think about at all. They squatted in a bleak wood and drank ditchwater strained through a rag. He'd seen the boy in a dream laid out upon a coolingboard and woke in horror. What he could bear in the waking world he could not by night and he sat awake for fear the dream would return.

They scrabbled through the charred ruins of houses they would not have entered before. A corpse floating in the black water of a basement among the trash and rusting duct-work. He stood in a livingroom partly burned and open to the sky. The waterbuckled boards sloping away into the yard. Soggy volumes in a bookcase. He took one down and opened it and then put it back. Everything damp. Rotting. In a drawer he found a candle. No way to light it. He put it in his pocket. He walked out in the gray light and stood and he saw for a brief moment the absolute truth of the world. The cold relentless circling of the intestate earth. Darkness implacable. The blind dogs of the sun in their running. The crushing black vacuum of the universe. And somewhere two hunted animals trembling like ground-foxes in their cover. Borrowed time and borrowed world and borrowed eyes with which to sorrow it.

At the edge of a small town they sat in the cab of a truck to rest, staring out a glass washed clean by the recent rains. A light dusting of ash. Exhausted. By the roadside stood another sign that warned of death, the letters faded with the years. He almost smiled. Can you read that? he said.

Yes.

Dont pay any attention. There's no one here.

Are they dead?

I think so.

I wish that little boy was with us.

Let's go, he said.

Rich dreams now which he was loathe to wake from. Things no longer known in the world. The cold drove him forth to mend the fire. Memory of her crossing the lawn toward the house in the early morning in a thin rose gown that clung to her breasts. He thought each memory recalled must do some violence to its origins. As in a party game. Say the word and pass it on. So be sparing. What you alter in the remembering has yet a reality, known or not.

They walked through the streets wrapped in the filthy blankets. He held the pistol at his waist and held the boy by the hand. At the farther edge of the town they came upon a solitary house in a field and they crossed and entered and walked through the rooms. They came upon themselves in a mirror and he almost raised the pistol. It's us, Papa, the boy whispered. It's us.

. . .

He stood in the back door and looked out at the fields and the road beyond and the bleak country beyond the road. On the patio was a barbeque pit made from a fifty-five gallon drum slit endways with a torch and set in a welded iron frame. A few dead trees in the yard. A fence. A metal tool shed. He shrugged off the blanket and wrapped it around the boy's shoulder.

I want you to wait here.

I want to go with you.

I'm only going over there to take a look. Just sit here. You'll be able to see me the whole time. I promise.

He crossed the yard and pushed open the door, still holding the gun. It was a sort of garden shed. Dirt floor. Metal shelves with some plastic flowerpots. Everything covered with ash. There were garden tools standing in the corner. A lawnmower. A wooden bench under the window and beside it a metal cabinet. He opened the cabinet. Old catalogs. Packets of seed. Begonia. Morning glory. He stuck them in his pocket. For what? On the top shelf were two cans of motor oil and he put the pistol in his belt and reached and got them and set them on the bench. They were very old, made of cardboard with metal endcaps. The oil had soaked through the cardboard but still they seemed full. He stepped back and looked out the door. The boy was sitting on the back steps of the house wrapped in the blankets watching him. When he turned he saw a gascan in the corner behind the door. He knew it couldnt have gas in it yet when he tilted it with his foot and let it fall back again there was a gentle slosh. He picked it up and carried it to the bench and tried to unscrew the cap but he could not. He got the pliers out of his coat pocket and extended the jaws and tried it. It would just fit and he twisted off the cap and laid it on the bench and sniffed the can. Rank odor. Years old. But it was gasoline and it would burn. He screwed the cap back on and put the pliers in his pocket. He looked around for some smaller container but there wasnt one. He shouldnt have thrown away the bottle. Check the house.

Crossing the grass he felt half faint and he had to stop. He wondered if it was from smelling the gasoline. The boy was watching him. How many days to death? Ten? Not so many more than that. He couldnt think. Why had he stopped? He turned and looked down at the grass. He walked back. Testing the ground with his feet. He stopped and turned again. Then he went back to the shed. He returned with a garden spade and in the place where he'd stood he chucked the blade into the ground. It sank to half its length and stopped with a hollow wooden sound. He began to shovel away the dirt.

Slow going. God he was tired. He leaned on the spade. He raised his head and looked at the boy. The boy sat as before. He bent to his work again. Before long he was resting between each shovelful. What he finally unburied was a piece of plywood covered with roofingfelt. He shoveled out along the edges. It was a door perhaps three feet by six. At one end was a hasp with a padlock taped up in a plastic bag. He rested, holding on to the handle of the spade, his forehead in the crook of his arm. When he looked up again the boy was standing in the yard just a few feet from him. He was very scared. Dont open it, Papa, he whispered.

It's okay.

Please, Papa. Please.

It's okay.

No it's not.

He had his fists clutched at his chest and he was bobbing up and down with fear. The man dropped the shovel and put his arms around him. Come on, he said. Let's just go sit on the porch and rest a while.

Then can we go?

Let's just sit for a while.

Okay.

They sat wrapped in the blankets and looked out at the yard. They sat for a long time. He tried to explain to the boy that there was no one buried in the yard but the boy just started crying. After a while he even thought that maybe the child was right.

Let's just sit, he said. We wont even talk.

Okay.

They walked through the house again. He found a beer bottle and an old rag of a curtain and he tore an edge from the cloth and stuffed it down the neck of the bottle with a coathanger. This is our new lamp, he said.

How can we light it?

I found some gasoline in the shed. And some oil. I'll show you.

Okay.

Come on, the man said. Everything's okay. I promise.

But when he bent to see into the boy's face under the

hood of the blanket he very much feared that something was gone that could not be put right again.

They went out and crossed the yard to the shed. He set the bottle on the bench and he took a screwdriver and punched a hole in one of the cans of oil and then punched a smaller one to help it drain. He pulled the wick out of the bottle and poured the bottle about half full, old straight weight oil thick and gelid with the cold and a long time pouring. He twisted the cap off the gascan and he made a small paper spill from one of the seedpackets and poured gas into the bottle and put his thumb over the mouth and shook it. Then he poured some out into a clay dish and took the rag and stuffed it back into the bottle with the screw-driver. He took a piece of flint from his pocket and got the pair of pliers and struck the flint against the serrated jaw. He tried it a couple of times and then he stopped and poured more gasoline into the dish. This may flare up, he said. The boy nodded. He raked sparks into the dish and it bloomed into flame with a low whoosh. He reached and got the bottle and tilted it and lit the wick and blew out the flame in the dish and handed the smoking bottle to the boy. Here, he said. Take it.

What are we going to do?

Hold your hand in front of the flame. Dont let it go out.

He rose and took the pistol from his belt. This door looks like the other door, he said. But it's not. I know you're scared. That's okay. I think there may be things in there and we have to take a look. There's no place else to go. This is it. I want you to help me. If you dont want to hold the lamp you'll have to take the pistol.

I'll hold the lamp.

Okay. This is what the good guys do. They keep trying. They dont give up.

Okay.

He led the boy out into the yard trailing the black smoke from the lamp. He put the pistol in his belt and picked up the spade and began to chop the hasp out of the plywood. He wedged the corner of the blade under it and pried it up and then knelt and took hold of the lock and twisted the whole thing loose and pitched it into the grass. He pried the blade under the door and got his fingers under it and then stood and raised it up. Dirt went rattling down the boards. He looked at the boy. Are you all right? he said. The boy nodded mutely, holding the lamp in front of him. The man swung the door over and let it fall in the grass. Rough stairs carpentered out of two by tens leading down

145

into the darkness. He reached and took the lamp from the boy. He started to descend the stairs but then he turned and leaned and kissed the child on the forehead.

The bunker was walled with concrete block. A poured concrete floor laid over with kitchen tile. There were a couple of iron cots with bare springs, one against either wall, the mattress pads rolled up at the foot of them in army fashion. He turned and looked at the boy crouched above him blinking in the smoke rising up from the lamp and then he descended to the lower steps and sat and held the lamp out. Oh my God, he whispered. Oh my God.

What is it Papa?

Come down. Oh my God. Come down.

Crate upon crate of canned goods. Tomatoes, peaches, beans, apricots. Canned hams. Corned beef. Hundreds of gallons of water in ten gallon plastic jerry jugs. Paper towels, toiletpaper, paper plates. Plastic trashbags stuffed with blankets. He held his forehead in his hand. Oh my God, he said. He looked back at the boy. It's all right, he said. Come down.

Papa?

Come down. Come down and see.

He stood the lamp on the step and went up and took the boy by the hand. Come on, he said. It's all right.

What did you find?

I found everything. Everything. Wait till you see. He led him down the stairs and picked up the bottle and held the flame aloft. Can you see? he said. Can you see?

What is all this stuff, Papa?

It's food. Can you read it?

Pears. That says pears.

Yes. Yes it does. Oh yes it does.

There was just headroom for him to stand. He ducked under a lantern with a green metal shade hanging from a hook. He held the boy by the hand and they went along the rows of stenciled cartons. Chile, corn, stew, soup, spaghetti sauce. The richness of a vanished world. Why is this here? the boy said. Is it real?

Oh yes. It's real.

He pulled one of the boxes down and clawed it open and held up a can of peaches. It's here because someone thought it might be needed.

147

But they didnt get to use it.

No. They didnt.

They died.

Yes.

Is it okay for us to take it?

Yes. It is. They would want us to. Just like we would want them to.

They were the good guys?

Yes. They were.

Like us.

Like us. Yes.

So it's okay.

Yes. It's okay.

There were knives and plastic utensils and silverware and kitchen tools in a plastic box. A can opener. There were electric torches that didnt work. He found a box of batteries and dry cells and went through them. Mostly corroded and leaking an acid goo but some of them looked okay. He finally got one of the lanterns to work and he set it on the table and blew out the smoky flame of the lamp. He tore a flap from the opened cardboard box and chased out the smoke with it and then he climbed up and lowered the trap door and turned and looked at the boy. What would you like for supper? he said.

Pears.

Good choice. Pears it is.

He took two paperware bowls from a stack of them wrapped in plastic and set them out on the table. He unrolled the mattress pads on the bunks for them to sit on and he opened the carton of pears and took out a can and set it on the table and clamped the lid with the can opener and began to turn the wheel. He looked at the boy. The boy was sitting quietly on the bunk, still wrapped in the blanket, watching. The man thought he had probably not fully committed himself to any of this. You could wake in the dark wet woods at any time. These will be the best pears you ever tasted, he said. The best. Just you wait.

They sat side by side and ate the can of pears. Then they ate a can of peaches. They licked the spoons and tipped the bowls and drank the rich sweet syrup. They looked at each other.

One more.

I dont want you to get sick.

I wont get sick.

You havent eaten in a long time.

I know.

Okay.

He put the boy to bed in the bunk and smoothed his filthy hair on the pillow and covered him with blankets. When he climbed up and lifted the door it was almost dark out. He went to the garage and got the knapsack and came back and took a last look around and then went down the steps and pulled the door shut and jammed one of the handles of the pliers through the heavy inside hasp. The electric lantern was already beginning to dim and he looked through the stores until he found some cases of white gas in gallon cans. He got one of the cans out and set it on the table and unscrewed the cap and punched out the metal seal with a screwdriver. Then he took down the lamp from the hook overhead and filled it. He'd already found a plastic box of butane lighters and he lit the lamp with one of them and adjusted the flame and hung it back up. Then he just sat on the bunk.

While the boy slept he began to go methodically through the stores. Clothes, sweaters, socks. A stainless steel basin and sponges and bars of soap. Toothpaste and toothbrushes. In the bottom of a big plastic jar of bolts and screws and miscellaneous hardware he found a double handful of gold krugerrands in a cloth sack. He dumped them out and kneaded them in his hand and looked at them and then scooped them back into the jar along with the hardware and put the jar back on the shelf.

He sorted through everything, shifting boxes and crates from one side of the room to the other. There was a small steel door that led into a second room where bottles of gas were stored. In the corner a chemical toilet. There were vent pipes in the walls covered with wire mesh and there were drains in the floor. It was getting warm in the bunker and he'd taken off his coat. He went through everything. He found a box of .45 ACP cartridges and three boxes of .30-30 rifle shells. What he didnt find was a gun. He took the battery lantern and walked over the floor and he checked the walls for any hidden compartment. After a while he just sat on the bunk eating a bar of chocolate. There was no gun and there wasnt going to be one.

. . .

When he woke the gaslamp overhead was hissing softly. The bunker walls were there in the light and the boxes and crates. He didnt know where he was. He was lying with his coat over him. He sat up and looked at the boy asleep on the other bunk. He'd taken off his shoes but he didnt remember that either and he got them from under the bunk and pulled them on and climbed the stairs and pulled the pliers from the hasp and lifted the door and peered out. Early morning. He looked at the house and he looked out toward the road and he was about to lower the hatch door again when he stopped. The vague gray light was in the west. They'd slept the night through and the day that followed. He lowered the door and secured it again and climbed back down and sat on the bunk. He looked around at the supplies. He'd been ready to die and now he wasnt going to and he had to think about that. Anyone could see the hatch lying in the yard and they would know at once what it was. He had to think about what to do. This was not hiding in the woods. This was the last thing from that. Finally he rose and went to the table and hooked up the little two burner gas stove and lit it and got out a frying pan and a kettle and opened the plastic box of kitchen implements.

· · ·

What woke the boy was him grinding coffee in a small hand grinder. He sat up and stared all around. Papa? he said.

Hi. Are you hungry?

I have to go to the bathroom. I have to pee.

He pointed with the spatula toward the low steel door. He didnt know how to use the toilet but they would use it anyway. They werent going to be here that long and he wasnt going to be opening and closing the hatch any more than they had to. The boy went past, his hair matted with sweat. What is that? he said.

Coffee. Ham. Biscuits.

Wow, the boy said.

He dragged a footlocker across the floor between the bunks and covered it with a towel and set out the plates and cups and plastic utensils. He set out a bowl of biscuits covered with a handtowel and a plate of butter and a can of condensed milk. Salt and pepper. He looked at the boy. The boy looked drugged. He brought the frying pan from the stove and forked a piece of browned ham onto the boy's plate and scooped scrambled eggs from the other pan and ladled out spoonfuls of baked beans and poured coffee into their cups. The boy looked up at him.

Go ahead, he said. Dont let it get cold.

What do I eat first?

Whatever you like.

Is this coffee?

Yes. Here. You put the butter on your biscuits. Like this.

Okay.

Are you all right?

I dont know.

Do you feel okay?

Yes.

What is it?

Do you think we should thank the people?

The people?

The people who gave us all this.

Well. Yes, I guess we could do that.

Will you do it?

Why dont you?

I dont know how.

Yes you do. You know how to say thank you.

The boy sat staring at his plate. He seemed lost. The man was about to speak when he said: Dear people, thank you for all this food and stuff. We know that you saved it for yourself and if you were here we wouldnt eat it no matter how hungry we were and we're sorry that you didnt get to eat it and we hope that you're safe in heaven with God.

He looked up. Is that okay? he said.

Yes. I think that's okay.

He wouldnt stay in the bunker by himself. He followed the man back and forth across the lawn while he carried the plastic jugs of water to the bathroom at the rear of the house. They took the little stove with them and a couple of pans and he heated water and poured it into the tub and poured in water from the plastic jugs. It took a long time but he wanted it to be good and warm. When the tub was almost full the boy got undressed and stepped shivering into the water and sat. Scrawny and filthy and naked. Holding his shoulders. The only light was from the ring of blue teeth in the burner of the stove. What do you think? the man said.

Warm at last.

Warm at last?

Yes.

Where did you get that?

I dont know.

Okay. Warm at last.

He washed his dirty matted hair and bathed him with the soap and sponges. He drained away the filthy water he sat in and laved fresh warm water over him from the pan and wrapped him shivering in a towel and wrapped him again in a blanket. He combed his hair and looked at him. Steam was coming off of him like smoke. Are you okay? he said.

My feet are cold.

You'll have to wait for me.

Hurry.

He bathed and then climbed out and poured detergent into the bathwater and shoved their stinking jeans down into the water with a toilet plunger. Are you ready? he said.

Yes.

He turned down the burner until it sputtered and went out and then he turned on the flashlight and laid it in the floor. They sat on the edge of the tub and pulled their shoes on and then he handed the boy the pan and soap and he took the stove and the little bottle of gas and the pistol and wrapped in their blankets they went back across the yard to the bunker.

They sat on the cot with a checkerboard between them, wearing new sweaters and socks and swaddled in the new blankets. He'd hooked up a small gas heater and they drank Coca Cola out of plastic mugs and after a while he went back to the house and wrung the water out of the jeans and brought them back and hung them to dry.

How long can we stay here Papa?

Not long.

How long is that?

I dont know. Maybe one more day. Two.

Because it's dangerous.

Yes.

Do you think they'll find us?

No. They wont find us.

They might find us.

No they wont. They wont find us.

Later when the boy was asleep he went to the house and dragged some of the furniture out onto the lawn. Then

157

he dragged out a mattress and laid it over the hatch and from inside he pulled it up over the plywood and carefully lowered the door so that the mattress covered it completely. It wasnt much of a ruse but it was better than nothing. While the boy slept he sat on the bunk and by the light of the lantern he whittled fake bullets from a treebranch with his knife, fitting them carefully into the empty bores of the cylinder and then whittling again. He shaped the ends with the knife and sanded them smooth with salt and he stained them with soot until they were the color of lead. When he had all five of them done he fitted them to the bores and snapped the cylinder shut and turned the gun and looked at it. Even this close the gun looked as if it were loaded and he laid it by and got up to feel the legs of the jeans steaming above the heater.

He'd saved the small handful of empty cartridge casings for the pistol but they were gone with everything else. He should have kept them in his pocket. He'd even lost the last one. He thought he might have been able to reload them out of the .45 cartridges. The primers would probably fit if he could get them out without ruining them. Shave the bullets to size with the boxcutter. He got up

158

and made a last tour of the stores. Then he turned down the lamp until the flame puttered out and he kissed the boy and crawled into the other bunk under the clean blankets and gazed one more time at this tiny paradise trembling in the orange light from the heater and then he fell asleep.

The town had been abandoned years ago but they walked the littered streets carefully, the boy holding on to his hand. They passed a metal trashdump where someone had once tried to burn bodies. The charred meat and bones under the damp ash might have been anonymous save for the shapes of the skulls. No longer any smell. There was a market at the end of the street and in one of the aisles piled with empty boxes there were three metal grocery carts. He looked them over and pulled one of them free and squatted and turned the wheels and then stood and pushed it up the aisle and back again.

We could take two of them, the boy said.

No.

I could push one.

You're the scout. I need you to be our lookout.

What are we going to do with all the stuff?

We'll just have to take what we can.

Do you think somebody is coming?

Yes. Sometime.

You said nobody was coming.

I didnt mean ever.

I wish we could live here.

I know.

We could be on the lookout.

We are on the lookout.

What if some good guys came?

Well, I dont think we're likely to meet any good guys on the road.

We're on the road.

I know.

If you're on the lookout all the time does that mean that you're scared all the time?

Well. I suppose you have to be scared enough to be on the lookout in the first place. To be cautious. Watchful.

But the rest of the time you're not scared?

The rest of the time.

Yeah.

I dont know. Maybe you should always be on the lookout. If trouble comes when you least expect it then maybe the thing to do is to always expect it.

Do you always expect it? Papa?

I do. But sometimes I might forget to be on the lookout.

He sat the boy on the footlocker under the gaslamp and with a plastic comb and a pair of scissors he set about cutting his hair. He tried to do a good job and it took some time. When he was done he took the towel from around the boy's shoulders and he scooped the golden hair from the floor and wiped the boy's face and shoulders with a damp cloth and held a mirror for him to see.

You did a good job, Papa.

Good.

I look really skinny.

You are really skinny.

He cut his own hair but it didnt come out so good. He trimmed his beard with the scissors while a pan of water heated and then he shaved himself with a plastic safety razor. The boy watched. When he was done he regarded himself in the mirror. He seemed to have no chin. He turned to the boy. How do I look? The boy cocked his head. I dont know, he said. Will you be cold?

. . .

They ate a sumptuous meal by candlelight. Ham and green beans and mashed potatoes with biscuits and gravy. He'd found four quarts of bonded whiskey still in the paper bags in which they'd been purchased and he drank a little of it in a glass with water. It made him dizzy before he'd even finished it and he drank no more. They ate peaches and cream over biscuits for dessert and drank coffee. The paper plates and plastic tableware he dumped in a trash-bag. Then they played checkers and then he put the boy to bed.

In the night he was wakened by the muted patter of rain on the mattress over the door above them. He thought it must be raining pretty hard for him to hear it. He got up with the flashlight and climbed up and raised the hatch and played the light across the yard. The yard was already flooded and the rain was slashing down. He closed the hatch. Water had leaked in and dripped down the stairs but he thought the bunker itself seemed pretty watertight. He went to see about the boy. He was damp with sweat and the man pulled back one of the blankets and fanned his face and then turned down the heater and went back to bed.

· · ·

When he woke again he thought the rain had stopped. But that wasnt what woke him. He'd been visited in a dream by creatures of a kind he'd never seen before. They did not speak. He thought that they'd been crouching by the side of his cot as he slept and then had skulked away on his awakening. He turned and looked at the boy. Maybe he understood for the first time that to the boy he was himself an alien. A being from a planet that no longer existed. The tales of which were suspect. He could not construct for the child's pleasure the world he'd lost without constructing the loss as well and he thought perhaps the child had known this better than he. He tried to remember the dream but he could not. All that was left was the feeling of it. He thought perhaps they'd come to warn him. Of what? That he could not enkindle in the heart of the child what was ashes in his own. Even now some part of him wished they'd never found this refuge. Some part of him always wished it to be over.

He checked the valve on the tank that it was turned off and swung the little stove around on the footlocker and sat and went to work dismantling it. He unscrewed the bottom panel and he removed the burner assembly and disconnected the two burners with a small crescent wrench. He tipped out the plastic jar of hardware and sorted out a bolt to thread into the fitting of the junction and then tightened it down. He connected the hose from the tank and held the little potmetal burner up in his hand, small and lightweight. He set it on the locker and carried the sheetmetal over and put it in the trash and went to the stairs to check the weather. The mattress on top of the hatch had soaked up a good deal of water and the door was hard to lift. He stood with it resting on his shoulders and looked out at the day. A light drizzle falling. Impossible to tell what time of the day he was looking at. He looked at the house and he looked out over the dripping countryside and then let the door back down and descended the steps and set about making breakfast.

They spent the day eating and sleeping. He'd planned to leave but the rain was justification enough to stay. The grocery cart was in the shed. Not likely that anyone would travel the road today. They sorted through the stores and set out what they could take, making of it a measured cube in the corner of the shelter. The day was brief, hardly a day at all. By dark the rain had ceased and they opened the hatch and began to carry boxes and parcels and plastic bags across the wet yard to the shed and to pack the cart. The faintly lit hatchway lay in the dark of the yard like a grave yawning at judgment day in some old apocalyptic painting. When the cart was loaded with all that it could hold he tied a plastic tarp down over it and fastened the grommets to the wire with short bungee cords and they stood back and looked at it with the flashlight. He thought that he should have gotten a couple of extra sets of wheels from the other carts in the store but it was too late now. He should have saved the motorcycle mirror off their old cart too. They ate dinner and slept till morning and then bathed again with sponges and washed their hair in basins of warm water. They ate breakfast and by first light they were on the road, wearing fresh masks cut from sheeting, the boy going ahead with a broom and clearing the way of sticks and branches and the man bent over the handle of the cart watching the road fall away before them.

The cart was too heavy to push into the wet woods and they nooned in the middle of the road and fixed hot tea and ate the last of the canned ham with crackers and with mustard and applesauce. Sitting back to back and watching the road. Do you know where we are Papa? the boy said.

Sort of.

How sort of?

Well. I think we're about two hundred miles from the coast. As the crow flies.

As the crow flies?

Yes. It means going in a straight line.

Are we going to get there soon?

Not real soon. Pretty soon. We're not going as the crow flies.

Because crows dont have to follow roads?

Yes.

They can go wherever they want.

Yes.

Do you think there might be crows somewhere?

I dont know.

But what do you think?

I think it's unlikely.

Could they fly to Mars or someplace?

No. They couldnt.

Because it's too far?

Yes.

Even if they wanted to.

Even if they wanted to.

What if they tried and they just got half way or something and then they were too tired. Would they fall back down?

Well. They really couldnt get half way because they'd be in space and there's not any air in space so they wouldnt be able to fly and besides it would be too cold and they'd freeze to death.

Oh.

Anyway they wouldnt know where Mars was.

Do we know where Mars is?

Sort of.

If we had a spaceship could we go there?

Well. If you had a really good spaceship and you had people to help you I suppose you could go.

Would there be food and stuff when you got there?

No. There's nothing there.

Oh.

They sat for a long time. They sat on their folded blankets and watched the road in both directions. No wind. Nothing. After a while the boy said: There's not any crows. Are there?

No.

Just in books.

Yes. Just in books.

I didnt think so.

Are you ready?

Yes.

They rose and put away their cups and the rest of the crackers. The man piled the blankets on top of the cart and fastened the tarp down and then he stood looking at the boy. What? the boy said.

I know you thought we were going to die.

Yeah.

But we didnt.

No.

Okay.

Can I ask you something?

Sure.

If you were a crow could you fly up high enough to see the sun?

Yes. You could.

I thought so. That would be really neat.

Yes it would. Are you ready?

Yes.

He stopped. What happened to your flute?

I threw it away.

You threw it away?

Yes.

Okay.

Okay.

In the long gray dusk they crossed a river and stopped
and looked down from the concrete balustrade at the slow
dead water passing underneath. Sketched upon the pall of
soot downstream the outline of a burnt city like a black
paper scrim. They saw it again just at dark pushing the
heavy cart up a long hill and they stopped to rest and
he turned the cart sideways in the road against it rolling.
Their masks were already gray at the mouth and their eyes
darkly cupped. They sat in the ashes by the side of the road
and looked out to the east where the shape of the city was
darkening into the coming night. They saw no lights.

Do you think there's anyone there, Papa?

I dont know.

How soon can we stop?

We can stop now.

On the hill?

We can get the cart down to those rocks and cover it with limbs.

Is this a good place to stop?

Well, people dont like to stop on hills. And we dont like for people to stop.

So it's a good place for us.

I think so.

Because we're smart.

Well, let's not get too smart.

Okay.

Are you ready?

Yes.

The boy stood up and got his broom and put it over his shoulder. He looked at his father. What are our long term goals? he said.

What?

Our long term goals.

Where did you hear that?

I dont know.

No, where did you?

You said it.

When?

A long time ago.

What was the answer?

I dont know.

Well. I dont either. Come on. It's getting dark.

Late in the day following as they rounded a bend in the road the boy stopped and put his hand on the carriage. Papa, he whispered. The man looked up. A small figure distant on the road, bent and shuffling.

He stood leaning on the handle of the grocery cart. Well, he said. Who's this?

What should we do, Papa?

It could be a decoy.

What are we going to do?

Let's just follow. We'll see if he turns around.

Okay.

The traveler was not one for looking back. They followed him for a while and then they overtook him. An old man, small and bent. He carried on his back an old army rucksack with a blanket roll tied across the top of it and he tapped along with a peeled stick for a cane. When he saw them he veered to the side of the road and turned and stood warily. He had a filthy towel tied under his jaw as if he suffered from toothache and even by their new world standards he smelled terrible.

I dont have anything, he said. You can look if you want.

We're not robbers.

He leaned one ear forward. What? he called.

I said we're not robbers.

What are you?

They'd no way to answer the question. He wiped his nose with the back of his wrist and stood waiting. He had no shoes at all and his feet were wrapped in rags and cardboard tied with green twine and any number of layers of vile clothing showed through the tears and holes in it. Of a sudden he seemed to wilt even further. He leaned on his cane and lowered himself into the road where he sat among the ashes with one hand over his head. He looked like a pile of rags fallen off a cart. They came forward and stood looking down at him. Sir? the man said. Sir?

The boy squatted and put a hand on his shoulder. He's scared, Papa. The man is scared.

He looked up the road and down. If this is an ambush he goes first, he said.

He's just scared, Papa.

Tell him we wont hurt him.

172

The old man shook his head from side to side, his fingers laced in his filthy hair. The boy looked up at his father.

Maybe he thinks we're not real.

What does he think we are?

I dont know.

We cant stay here. We have to go.

He's scared, Papa.

I dont think you should touch him.

Maybe we could give him something to eat.

He stood looking off down the road. Damn, he whispered. He looked down at the old man. Perhaps he'd turn into a god and they to trees. All right, he said.

He untied the tarp and folded it back and rummaged through the canned goods and came up with a tin of fruit cocktail and took the can opener from his pocket and opened the tin and folded back the lid and walked over and squatted and handed it to the boy.

What about a spoon?

He's not getting a spoon.

The boy took the tin and handed it to the old man. Take it, he whispered. Here.

The old man raised his eyes and looked at the boy. The

boy gestured at him with the tin. He looked like someone trying to feed a vulture broken in the road. It's okay, he
said.

The old man lowered his hand from his head. He
blinked. Grayblue eyes half buried in the thin and sooty
creases of his skin.

Take it, the boy said.

He reached with his scrawny claws and took it and held
it to his chest.

Eat it, the boy said. It's good. He made tipping motions
with his hands. The old man looked down at the tin.
He took a fresh grip and lifted it, his nose wrinkling. His
long and yellowed claws scrabbled at the metal. Then he
tipped it and drank. The juice ran down his filthy beard.
He lowered the can, chewing with difficulty. He jerked his
head when he swallowed. Look, Papa, the boy whispered.

I see, the man said.

The boy turned and looked at him.

I know what the question is, the man said. The answer is
no.

What's the question?

Can we keep him. We cant.

I know.

You know.

174

Yeah.

All right.

Can we give him something else?

Let's see how he does with this.

They watched him eat. When he was done he sat holding the empty tin and looking down into it as if more might appear.

What do you want to give him?

What do you think he should have?

I dont think he should have anything. What do you want to give him?

We could cook something on the stove. He could eat with us.

You're talking about stopping. For the night.

Yeah.

He looked down at the old man and he looked at the road. All right, he said. But then tomorrow we go on.

The boy didnt answer.

That's the best deal you're going to get.

Okay.

Okay means okay. It doesnt mean we negotiate another deal tomorrow.

What's negotiate?

It means talk about it some more and come up with some other deal. There is no other deal. This is it.

Okay.

Okay.

They helped the old man to his feet and handed him his cane. He didnt weigh a hundred pounds. He stood looking about uncertainly. The man took the tin from him and slung it into the woods. The old man tried to hand him the cane but he pushed it away. When did you eat last? he said.

I dont know.

You dont remember.

I ate just now.

Do you want to eat with us?

I dont know.

You dont know?

Eat what?

Maybe some beef stew. With crackers. And coffee.

What do I have to do?

Tell us where the world went.

What?

You dont have to do anything. Can you walk okay?

I can walk.

He looked down at the boy. Are you a little boy? he said.

The boy looked at his father.

What does he look like? his father said.

I dont know. I cant see good.

Can you see me?

I can tell someone's there.

Good. We need to get going. He looked at the boy. Dont hold his hand, he said.

He cant see.

Dont hold his hand. Let's go.

Where are we going? the old man said.

We're going to eat.

He nodded and reached out with his cane and tapped tentatively at the road.

How old are you?

I'm ninety.

No you're not.

Okay.

Is that what you tell people?

What people?

Any people.

I guess so.

So they wont hurt you?

Yes.

Does that work?

No.

What's in your pack?

Nothing. You can look.

I know I can look. What's in there?

Nothing. Just some stuff.

Nothing to eat.

No.

What's your name?

Ely.

Ely what?

What's wrong with Ely?

Nothing. Let's go.

They bivouacked in the woods much nearer to the road than he would have liked. He had to drag the cart while the boy steered from behind and they built a fire for the old man to warm himself though he didnt much like that either. They ate and the old man sat wrapped in his solitary quilt and gripped his spoon like a child. They had only two cups and he drank his coffee from the bowl he'd eaten from, his thumbs hooked over the rim. Sitting like a starved and threadbare buddha, staring into the coals.

You cant go with us, you know, the man said.

He nodded.

How long have you been on the road?

I was always on the road. You cant stay in one place.

How do you live?

I just keep going. I knew this was coming.

You knew it was coming?

Yeah. This or something like it. I always believed in it.

Did you try to get ready for it?

No. What would you do?

I dont know.

People were always getting ready for tomorrow. I didnt believe in that. Tomorrow wasnt getting ready for them. It didnt even know they were there.

I guess not.

Even if you knew what to do you wouldnt know what to do. You wouldnt know if you wanted to do it or not. Suppose you were the last one left? Suppose you did that to yourself?

Do you wish you would die?

No. But I might wish I had died. When you're alive you've always got that ahead of you.

Or you might wish you'd never been born.

Well. Beggars cant be choosers.

You think that would be asking too much.

What's done is done. Anyway, it's foolish to ask for luxuries in times like these.

I guess so.

Nobody wants to be here and nobody wants to leave. He lifted his head and looked across the fire at the boy. Then he looked at the man. The man could see his small eyes watching him in the firelight. God knows what those eyes saw. He got up to pile more wood on the fire and he raked the coals back from the dead leaves. The red sparks rose in a shudder and died in the blackness overhead. The old man drank the last of his coffee and set the bowl before him and leaned toward the heat with his hands out. The man watched him. How would you know if you were the last man on earth? he said.

I dont guess you would know it. You'd just be it.

Nobody would know it.

It wouldnt make any difference. When you die it's the same as if everybody else did too.

I guess God would know it. Is that it?

There is no God.

No?

There is no God and we are his prophets.

I dont understand how you're still alive. How do you eat?

I dont know.

You dont know?

People give you things.

People give you things.

Yes.

To eat.

To eat. Yes.

No they dont.

You did.

No I didnt. The boy did.

There's other people on the road. You're not the only ones.

Are you the only one?

The old man peered warily. What do you mean? he said.

Are there people with you?

What people?

Any people.

There's not any people. What are you talking about?

I'm talking about you. About what line of work you might be in.

The old man didnt answer.

I suppose you want to go with us.

Go with you.

Yes.

You wont take me with you.

You dont want to go.

I wouldnt have even come this far but I was hungry.

The people that gave you food. Where are they?

There's not any people. I just made that up.

What else did you make up?

I'm just on the road the same as you. No different.

Is your name really Ely?

No.

You dont want to say your name.

I dont want to say it.

Why?

I couldnt trust you with it. To do something with it. I dont want anybody talking about me. To say where I was or what I said when I was there. I mean, you could talk about me maybe. But nobody could say that it was me. I could be anybody. I think in times like these the less said the better. If something had happened and we were survivors and we met on the road then we'd have something to talk about. But we're not. So we dont.

Maybe not.

You just dont want to say in front of the boy.

You're not a shill for a pack of roadagents?

I'm not anything. I'll leave if you want me to. I can find the road.

You dont have to leave.

I've not seen a fire in a long time, that's all. I live like an animal. You dont want to know the things I've eaten. When I saw that boy I thought that I had died.

You thought he was an angel?

I didnt know what he was. I never thought to see a child again. I didnt know that would happen.

What if I said that he's a god?

The old man shook his head. I'm past all that now. Have been for years. Where men cant live gods fare no better. You'll see. It's better to be alone. So I hope that's not true what you said because to be on the road with the last god would be a terrible thing so I hope it's not true. Things will be better when everybody's gone.

They will?

Sure they will.

Better for who?

Everybody.

Everybody.

Sure. We'll all be better off. We'll all breathe easier.

That's good to know.

Yes it is. When we're all gone at last then there'll be nobody here but death and his days will be numbered too. He'll be out in the road there with nothing to do and nobody to do it to. He'll say: Where did everybody go? And that's how it will be. What's wrong with that?

In the morning they stood in the road and he and the boy argued about what to give the old man. In the end he didnt get much. Some cans of vegetables and of fruit. Finally the boy just went over to the edge of the road and sat in the ashes. The old man fitted the tins into his knapsack and fastened the straps. You should thank him you know, the man said. I wouldnt have given you anything.

Maybe I should and maybe I shouldnt.

Why wouldnt you?

I wouldnt have given him mine.

You dont care if it hurts his feelings?

Will it hurt his feelings?

No. That's not why he did it.

Why did he do it?

He looked over at the boy and he looked at the old man. You wouldnt understand, he said. I'm not sure I do.

Maybe he believes in God.

I dont know what he believes in.

He'll get over it.

No he wont.

The old man didnt answer. He looked around at the day.

You wont wish us luck either, will you? the man said.

I dont know what that would mean. What luck would look like. Who would know such a thing?

Then all went on. When he looked back the old man had set out with his cane, tapping his way, dwindling slowly on the road behind them like some storybook peddler from an antique time, dark and bent and spider thin and soon to vanish forever. The boy never looked back at all.

In the early afternoon they spread their tarp on the road and sat and ate a cold lunch. The man watched him. Are you talking? he said.

Yes.

But you're not happy.

I'm okay.

When we're out of food you'll have more time to think about it.

The boy didnt answer. They ate. He looked back up the road. After a while he said: I know. But I wont remember it the way you do.

Probably not.

I didnt say you were wrong.

Even if you thought it.

It's okay.

Yeah, the man said. Well. There's not a lot of good news on the road. In times like these.

You shouldnt make fun of him.

Okay.

He's going to die.

I know.

Can we go now?

Yeah, the man said. We can go.

In the night he woke in the cold dark coughing and he coughed till his chest was raw. He leaned to the fire and blew on the coals and he put on more wood and rose and walked away from the camp as far as the light would carry him. He knelt in the dry leaves and ash with the blanket wrapped about his shoulders and after a while the coughing began to subside. He thought about the old man out there somewhere. He looked back at the camp through the black palings of the trees. He hoped the boy had gone back to sleep. He knelt there wheezing softly, his hands on his knees. I am going to die, he said. Tell me how I am to do that.

The day following they trekked on till almost dark. He could find no safe place to make a fire. When he lifted the tank from the cart he thought that it felt light. He sat and turned the valve but the valve was already on. He turned the little knob on the burner. Nothing. He leaned and listened. He tried both valves again in their combinations. The tank was empty. He squatted there with his hands folded into a fist against his forehead, his eyes closed. After a while he raised his head and just sat there staring out at the cold and darkening woods.

They ate a cold supper of cornbread and beans and franks from a tin. The boy asked him how the tank had gone empty so soon but he said that it just had.

You said it would last for weeks.

I know.

But it's just been a few days.

I was wrong.

They ate in silence. After a while the boy said: I forgot to turn off the valve, didnt I?

It's not your fault. I should have checked.

The boy set his plate down on the tarp. He looked away.

It's not your fault. You have to turn off both valves. The threads were supposed to be sealed with teflon tape or it would leak and I didnt do it. It's my fault. I didnt tell you.

There wasnt any tape though, was there?

It's not your fault.

They plodded on, thin and filthy as street addicts. Cowled in their blankets against the cold and their breath smoking, shuffling through the black and silky drifts. They were crossing the broad coastal plain where the secular winds drove them in howling clouds of ash to find shelter where they could. Houses or barns or under the bank of a roadside ditch with the blankets pulled over their heads and the noon sky black as the cellars of hell. He held the boy against him, cold to the bone. Dont lose heart, he said. We'll be all right.

· · ·

The land was gullied and eroded and barren. The bones of dead creatures sprawled in the washes. Middens of anonymous trash. Farmhouses in the fields scoured of their paint and the clapboards spooned and sprung from the wallstuds. All of it shadowless and without feature. The road descended through a jungle of dead kudzu. A marsh where the dead reeds lay over the water. Beyond the edge of the fields the sullen haze hung over earth and sky alike. By late afternoon it had begun to snow and they went on with the tarp over them and the wet snow hissing on the plastic.

He'd slept little in weeks. When he woke in the morning the boy was not there and he sat up with the pistol in his hand and then stood and looked for him but he was not in sight. He pulled on his shoes and walked out to the edge of the trees. Bleak dawn in the east. The alien sun commencing its cold transit. He saw the boy coming at a run across the fields. Papa, he called. There's a train in the woods.

A train?

Yes.

A real train?

Yes. Come on.

You didnt go up to it did you?

No. Just a little. Come on.

There's nobody there?

No. I dont think so. I came to get you.

Is there an engine?

Yes. A big diesel.

They crossed the field and entered the woods on the far side. The tracks came down out of the country on a banked rise and ran through the woods. The locomotive was a diesel electric and there were eight stainless steel passenger coaches behind it. He took hold of the boy's hand. Let's just sit and watch, he said.

They sat on the embankment and waited. Nothing moved. He handed the pistol to the boy. You take it, Papa, the boy said.

No. That's not the deal. Take it.

He took the pistol and sat with it in his lap and the man went down the right of way and stood looking at the train. He crossed the tracks to the other side and walked down the length of the cars. When he came out from behind the last coach he waved for the boy to come and the boy rose and put the pistol in his belt.

Everything was covered in ash. The aisles littered. Suitcases stood open in the seats where they'd been lifted down from the overhead racks and rifled long ago. In the club car he found a stack of paper plates and he blew the dust from them and put them inside his parka and that was all.

How did it get here, Papa?

I dont know. I guess someone was taking it south. A group of people. This is probably where they ran out of fuel.

Has it been here for a long time?

Yes. I think so. A pretty long time.

They went through the last of the cars and then walked up the track to the locomotive and climbed up to the catwalk. Rust and scaling paint. They pushed into the cab and he blew away the ash from the engineer's seat and put the boy at the controls. The controls were very simple. Little to do but push the throttle lever forward. He made train noises and diesel horn noises but he wasnt sure what these might

mean to the boy. After a while they just looked out through
the silted glass to where the track curved away in the waste
of weeds. If they saw different worlds what they knew
was the same. That the train would sit there slowly decom-
posing for all eternity and that no train would ever run
again.

Can we go, Papa?

Yes. Of course we can.

They began to come upon from time to time small cairns of
rock by the roadside. They were signs in gypsy language,
lost patterans. The first he'd seen in some while, common
in the north, leading out of the looted and exhausted
cities, hopeless messages to loved ones lost and dead.
By then all stores of food had given out and murder was
everywhere upon the land. The world soon to be largely
populated by men who would eat your children in front
of your eyes and the cities themselves held by cores of
blackened looters who tunneled among the ruins and
crawled from the rubble white of tooth and eye carrying
charred and anonymous tins of food in nylon nets like
shoppers in the commissaries of hell. The soft black talc
blew through the streets like squid ink uncoiling along

a sea floor and the cold crept down and the dark came early and the scavengers passing down the steep canyons with their torches trod silky holes in the drifted ash that closed behind them silently as eyes. Out on the roads the pilgrims sank down and fell over and died and the bleak and shrouded earth went trundling past the sun and returned again as trackless and as unremarked as the path of any nameless sisterworld in the ancient dark beyond.

Long before they reached the coast their stores were all but gone. The country was stripped and plundered years ago and they found nothing in the houses and buildings by the roadside. He found a telephone directory in a filling station and he wrote the name of the town on their map with a pencil. They sat on the curb in front of the building and ate crackers and looked for the town but they couldnt find it. He sorted through the sections and looked again. Finally he showed the boy. They were some fifty miles west of where he'd thought. He drew stick figures on the map. This is us, he said. The boy traced the route to the sea with his finger. How long will it take us to get there? he said.

Two weeks. Three.

Is it blue?

The sea? I dont know. It used to be.

The boy nodded. He sat looking at the map. The man watched him. He thought he knew what that was about. He'd pored over maps as a child, keeping one finger on the town where he lived. Just as he would look up his family in the phone directory. Themselves among others, everything in its place. Justified in the world. Come on, he said. We should go.

In the late afternoon it began to rain. They left the road and took a dirt drive through a field and spent the night in a shed. The shed had a concrete floor and at the far end stood some empty steel drums. He blocked the doors with the drums and built a fire in the floor and he made beds out of some flattened cardboard boxes. The rain drummed all night on the steel roof overhead. When he woke the fire had burned down and it was very cold. The boy was sitting up wrapped in his blanket.

What is it?

Nothing. I had a bad dream.

What did you dream about?

Nothing.

Are you okay?

No.

He put his arms around him and held him. It's okay, he said.

I was crying. But you didnt wake up.

I'm sorry. I was just so tired.

I meant in the dream.

In the morning when he woke the rain had stopped. He listened to the slack drip of water. He shifted his hips on the hard concrete and looked out through the boards at the gray country. The boy was still sleeping. Water dripped in puddles in the floor. Small bubbles appeared and skated and vanished again. In a town in the piedmont they'd slept in a place like this and listened to the rain. There was an oldfashioned drugstore there with a black marble counter and chrome stools with tattered plastic seats patched with electrical tape. The pharmacy was looted but the store itself was oddly intact. Expensive electronic equipment sat unmolested on the shelves. He stood looking the place over. Sundries. Notions. What are these? He took the boy's hand and led him out but the boy had already seen it. A human head beneath a cakebell at the end of the counter.

Dessicated. Wearing a ballcap. Dried eyes turned sadly inward. Did he dream this? He did not. He rose and knelt and blew at the coals and dragged up the burned board ends and got the fire going.

There are other good guys. You said so.
Yes.
So where are they?
They're hiding.
Who are they hiding from?
From each other.
Are there lots of them?
We dont know.
But some.
Some. Yes.
Is that true?
Yes. That's true.
But it might not be true.
I think it's true.
Okay.
You dont believe me.
I believe you.

Okay.

I always believe you.

I dont think so.

Yes I do. I have to.

They hiked back down to the highway through the mud. Smell of earth and wet ash in the rain. Dark water in the roadside ditch. Sucking out of an iron culvert into a pool. In a yard a plastic deer. Late the day following they entered a small town where three men stepped from behind a truck and stood in the road before them. Emaciated, clothed in rags. Holding lengths of pipe. What have you got in the basket? He leveled the pistol at them. They stood. The boy clung to his coat. No one spoke. He set the cart forward again and they moved to the side of the road. He had the boy take the cart and he walked backwards keeping the pistol on them. He tried to look like any common migratory killer but his heart was hammering and he knew he was going to start coughing. They drifted back into the road and stood watching. He put the pistol in his belt and turned and took the cart. At the top of the rise when he looked back they were still standing there.

He told the boy to push the cart and he walked out through a yard to where he could see back down the road but now they were gone. The boy was very scared. He laid the gun on top of the tarp and took the cart and they went on.

They lay in a field until dark watching the road but no one came. It was very cold. When it was too dark to see they got the cart and stumbled back to the road and he got the blankets out and they wrapped themselves up and went on. Feeling out the paving under their feet. One wheel on the cart had developed a periodic squeak but there was nothing to be done about it. They struggled on for some hours and then floundered off through the roadside brush and lay shivering and exhausted on the cold ground and slept till day. When he woke he was sick.

He'd come down with a fever and they lay in the woods like fugitives. Nowhere to build a fire. Nowhere safe. The boy sat in the leaves watching him. His eyes brimming. Are you going to die, Papa? he said. Are you going to die?

No. I'm just sick.

I'm really scared.

I know. It's all right. I'm going to get better. You'll
see.

His dreams brightened. The vanished world returned. Kin
long dead washed up and cast fey sidewise looks upon
him. None spoke. He thought of his life. So long ago. A
gray day in a foreign city where he stood in a window and
watched the street below. Behind him on a wooden table a
small lamp burned. On the table books and papers. It had
begun to rain and a cat at the corner turned and crossed
the sidewalk and sat beneath the cafe awning. There was a
woman at a table there with her head in her hands. Years
later he'd stood in the charred ruins of a library where
blackened books lay in pools of water. Shelves tipped over.
Some rage at the lies arranged in their thousands row on
row. He picked up one of the books and thumbed through
the heavy bloated pages. He'd not have thought the value
of the smallest thing predicated on a world to come. It surprised him. That the space which these things occupied
was itself an expectation. He let the book fall and took a
last look around and made his way out into the cold gray
light.

. . .

Three days. Four. He slept poorly. The racking cough woke him. Rasping suck of air. I'm sorry, he said to the pitiless dark. It's okay said the boy.

He got the little oillamp lit and left it sitting on a rock and he rose and shuffled out through the leaves wrapped in his blankets. The boy whispered for him not to go. Just a little ways, he said. Not far. I'll hear you if you call. If the lamp should blow out he could not find his way back. He sat in the leaves at the top of the hill and looked into the blackness. Nothing to see. No wind. In the past when he walked out like that and sat looking over the country lying in just the faintest visible shape where the lost moon tracked the caustic waste he'd sometimes see a light. Dim and shapeless in the murk. Across a river or deep in the blackened quadrants of a burned city. In the morning sometimes he'd return with the binoculars and glass the countryside for any sign of smoke but he never saw any.

Standing at the edge of a winter field among rough men. The boy's age. A little older. Watching while they opened up the rocky hillside ground with pick and mattock and brought to light a great bolus of serpents perhaps a hundred in number. Collected there for a common warmth. The dull tubes of them beginning to move sluggishly in the cold hard light. Like the bowels of some great beast exposed to the day. The men poured gasoline on them and burned them alive, having no remedy for evil but only for the image of it as they conceived it to be. The burning snakes twisted horribly and some crawled burning across the floor of the grotto to illuminate its darker recesses. As they were mute there were no screams of pain and the men watched them burn and writhe and blacken in just such silence themselves and they disbanded in silence in the winter dusk each with his own thoughts to go home to their suppers.

One night the boy woke from a dream and would not tell him what it was.

You dont have to tell me, the man said. It's all right.

I'm scared.

It's all right.

No it's not.

It's just a dream.

I'm really scared.

I know.

The boy turned away. The man held him. Listen to me, he said.

What.

When your dreams are of some world that never was or of some world that never will be and you are happy again then you will have given up. Do you understand? And you cant give up. I wont let you.

When they set out again he was very weak and for all his speeches he'd become more faint of heart than he had been in years. Filthy with diarrhea, leaning on the bar handle of the shopping cart. He looked at the boy out of his sunken haggard eyes. Some new distance between them. He could feel it. In two day's time they came upon a country where firestorms had passed leaving mile on mile of burn. A cake of ash in the roadway inches deep and hard going with the cart. The blacktop underneath had buckled in the heat and then set back again. He leaned on the handle and looked down the long straight of way. The thin trees down. The waterways a gray sludge. A blackened jackstraw land.

. . .

Beyond a crossroads in that wilderness they began to come upon the possessions of travelers abandoned in the road years ago. Boxes and bags. Everything melted and black. Old plastic suitcases curled shapeless in the heat. Here and there the imprint of things wrested out of the tar by scavengers. A mile on and they began to come upon the dead. Figures half mired in the blacktop, clutching themselves, mouths howling. He put his hand on the boy's shoulder. Take my hand, he said. I dont think you should see this.

What you put in your head is there forever?

Yes.

It's okay Papa.

It's okay?

They're already there.

I dont want you to look.

They'll still be there.

He stopped and leaned on the cart. He looked down the road and he looked at the boy. So strangely untroubled.

Why dont we just go on, the boy said.

Yes. Okay.

They were trying to get away werent they Papa?

Yes. They were.

Why didnt they leave the road?

They couldnt. Everything was on fire.

They picked their way among the mummied figures. The black skin stretched upon the bones and their faces split and shrunken on their skulls. Like victims of some ghastly envacuuming. Passing them in silence down that silent corridor through the drifting ash where they struggled forever in the road's cold coagulate.

They passed through the site of a roadside hamlet burned to nothing. Some metal storage tanks, a few standing flues of blackened brick. There were gray slagpools of melted glass in the ditches and the raw lightwires lay in rusting skeins for miles along the edge of the roadway. He was coughing every step of it. He saw the boy watching him. He was what the boy thought about. Well should he.

They sat in the road and ate leftover skilletbread hard as biscuit and their last can of tunafish. He opened a can of prunes and they passed it between them. The boy held the tin up and drained the last of the juice and then sat with the tin in his lap and passed his forefinger around the inside of it and put his finger in his mouth.

Dont cut your finger, the man said.

You always say that.

I know.

He watched him lick the lid of the tin. With great care. Like a cat licking its reflection in a glass. Stop watching me, he said.

Okay.

He folded down the lid of the can and set it in the road before him. What? he said. What is it?

Nothing.

Tell me.

I think there's someone following us.

That's what I thought.

That's what you thought?

Yes. That's what I thought you were going to say. What do you want to do?

I dont know.

What do you think?

Let's just go. We should hide our trash.

Because they'll think we have lots of food.

Yes.

And they'll try to kill us.

They wont kill us.

They might try to.

We're okay.

Okay.

I think we should lay in the weeds for them. See who they are.

And how many.

And how many. Yes.

Okay.

If we can get across the creek we could go up on the bluffs there and watch the road.

Okay.

We'll find a place.

They rose and piled their blankets in the cart. Get the tin, the man said.

It was late into the long twilight before the road crossed the creek. They trundled over the bridge and pushed the cart out through the woods looking for some place to leave it where it would not be seen. They stood looking back at the road in the dusk.

What if we put it under the bridge? the boy said.

What if they go down there for water?

How far back do you think they are?

I dont know.

It's getting dark.

I know.

What if they go by in the dark?

Let's just find a place where we can watch. It's not dark yet.

They hid the cart and went up the slope among the rocks carrying their blankets and they dug themselves in where they could see back down the road through the trees for perhaps half a mile. They were sheltered from the wind and they wrapped themselves in their blankets and took turns watching but after a while the boy was asleep. He was almost asleep himself when he saw a figure appear at the top of the road and stand there. Soon two more appeared. Then a fourth. They stood and grouped. Then they came on. He could just make them out in the deep dusk. He thought they might stop soon and he wished he'd found a place further from the road. If they stopped at the bridge it would be a long cold night. They came down the road and crossed the bridge. Three men and a woman. The woman walked with a waddling gait and as she approached he could see that she was pregnant. The men carried packs on their backs and the woman carried a small cloth suitcase. All of them wretchedlooking beyond description. Their breath steaming softly. They crossed the bridge and continued on down the road and vanished one by one into the waiting darkness.

It was a long night anyway. When it was light enough to see he pulled on his shoes and rose and wrapped one of the blankets around him and walked out and stood looking at the road below. The bare ironcolored wood and the fields beyond. The corrugate shapes of old harrowtroughs still faintly visible. Cotton perhaps. The boy was sleeping and he went down to the cart and got the map and the bottle of water and a can of fruit from their small stores and he came back and sat in the blankets and studied the map.

You always think we've gone further than we have.
He moved his finger. Here then.
More.

Here.

Okay.

He folded up the limp and rotting pages. Okay, he said.

They sat looking out through the trees at the road.

Do you think that your fathers are watching? That they weigh you in their ledgerbook? Against what? There is no book and your fathers are dead in the ground.

The country went from pine to liveoak and pine. Magnolias. Trees as dead as any. He picked up one of the heavy leaves and crushed it in his hand to powder and let the powder sift through his fingers.

On the road early the day following. They'd not gone far when the boy pulled at his sleeve and they stopped and stood. A thin stem of smoke was rising out of the woods ahead. They stood watching.

What should we do, Papa?

Maybe we should take a look.

Let's just keep going.

What if they're going the same way we are?

So? the boy said.

We're going to have them behind us. I'd like to know who it is.

What if it's an army?

It's just a small fire.

Why dont we just wait?

We cant wait. We're almost out of food. We have to keep going.

They left the cart in the woods and he checked the rotation of the rounds in the cylinder. The wooden and the true. They stood listening. The smoke stood vertically in the still air. No sound of any kind. The leaves were soft from the recent rains and quiet underfoot. He turned and looked at the boy. The small dirty face wide with fear. They circled the fire at a distance, the boy holding on to his hand. He crouched and put his arm around him and they listened for a long time. I think they've gone, he whispered.

What?

I think they're gone. They probably had a lookout.

It could be a trap, Papa.

Okay. Let's wait a while.

They waited. They could see the smoke through the trees. A wind had begun to trouble the top of the spire and the smoke shifted and they could smell it. They could smell something cooking. Let's circle around, the man said.

Can I hold your hand?

Yes. Of course you can.

The woods were just burned trunks. There was nothing to see. I think they saw us, the man said. I think they saw us and ran away. They saw we had a gun.

They left their food cooking.

Yes.

Let's take a look.

It's really scary, Papa.

There's no one here. It's okay.

They walked into the little clearing, the boy clutching his hand. They'd taken everything with them except whatever black thing was skewered over the coals. He was standing there checking the perimeter when the boy turned and buried his face against him. He looked quickly to see what had happened. What is it? he said. What is it? The boy shook his head. Oh Papa, he said. He turned and looked again. What the boy had seen was a charred human infant headless and gutted and blackening on the spit. He bent and picked the boy up and started for the road with him, holding him close. I'm sorry, he whispered. I'm sorry.

He didnt know if he'd ever speak again. They camped at a river and he sat by the fire listening to the water running in the dark. It wasnt a safe place because the sound of the river masked any other but he thought it would cheer the boy up. They ate the last of their provisions and he sat studying the map. He measured the road with a piece of string and looked at it and measured again. Still a long way to the coast. He didnt know what they'd find when they got there. He shuffled the sections together and put them back in the plastic bag and sat staring into the coals.

The following day they crossed the river by a narrow iron bridge and entered an old mill town. They went through the wooden houses but they found nothing. A man sat on a porch in his coveralls dead for years. He looked a straw man set out to announce some holiday. They went down the long dark wall of the mill, the windows bricked up. The fine black soot raced along the street before them.

Odd things scattered by the side of the road. Electrical appliances, furniture. Tools. Things abandoned long ago by pilgrims enroute to their several and collective deaths. Even a year ago the boy might sometimes pick up something and carry it with him for a while but he didnt do that any more. They sat and rested and drank the last of their good water and left the plastic jerry jug standing in the road. The boy said: If we had that little baby it could go with us.

Yes. It could.

Where did they find it?

He didnt answer.

Could there be another one somewhere?

I dont know. It's possible.

I'm sorry about what I said about those people.

What people?

Those people that got burned up. That were struck in the road and got burned up.

I didnt know that you said anything bad.

It wasnt bad. Can we go now?

Okay. Do you want to ride in the cart?

It's okay.

Why dont you ride for while?

I dont want to. It's okay.

Slow water in the flat country. The sloughs by the roadside motionless and gray. The coastal plain rivers in leaden serpentine across the wasted farmland. They went on. Ahead in the road was a dip and a stand of cane. I think there's a bridge there, he said. Probably a creek.

Can we drink the water?

We dont have a choice.

It wont make us sick.

I dont think so. It could be dry.

Can I go ahead?

Yes. Of course you can.

The boy set off down the road. He'd not seen him run in a long time. Elbows out, flapping along in his outsized tennis shoes. He stopped and stood watching, biting his lip.

. . .

The water was little more than a seep. He could see it moving slightly where it drew down into a concrete tile under the roadway and he spat into the water and watched to see if it would move. He got a cloth from the cart and a plastic jar and came back and wrapped the cloth over the mouth of the jar and sank it in the water and watched it fill. He raised it up dripping and held it to the light. It didnt look too bad. He took the cloth away and handed the jar to the boy. Go ahead, he said.

The boy drank and handed it back.

Drink some more.

You drink some, Papa.

Okay.

They sat filtering the ash from the water and drinking until they could hold no more. The boy lay back in the grass.

We need to go.

I'm really tired.

I know.

He sat watching him. They'd not eaten in two days. In two more they would begin to get weak. He climbed the bank through the cane to check the road. Dark and black and trackless where it crossed the open country. The winds had swept the ash and dust from the surface. Rich lands at one time. No sign of life anywhere. It was no country that he knew. The names of the towns or the rivers. Come on, he said. We have to go.

They slept more and more. More than once they woke sprawled in the road like traffic victims. The sleep of death. He sat up reaching about for the pistol. In the leaden evening he stood leaning with his elbows on the cart handle and looking across the fields at a house perhaps a mile away. It was the boy who had seen it. Shifting in and out of the curtain of soot like a house in some uncertain dream. He leaned on the cart and looked at him. It would cost them some effort to get there. Take their blankets. Hide the cart someplace along the road. They could reach it before dark but they couldnt get back.

We have to take a look. We have no choice.

I dont want to.

We havent eaten in days.

I'm not hungry.

No, you're starving.

I dont want to go there Papa.

There's no one there. I promise.

How do you know?

I just know.

They could be there.

No they're not. It will be okay.

They set out across the fields wrapped in their blankets, carrying only the pistol and a bottle of water. The field had been turned a last time and there were stalks of stubble sticking out of the ground and the faint trace of the disc was still visible from east to west. It had rained recently and the earth was soft underfoot and he kept his eye on the ground and before long he stopped and picked up an arrowhead. He spat on it and wiped away the dirt on the seam of his trousers and gave it to the boy. It was white quartz, perfect as the day it was made. There are more, he said. Watch the ground, you'll see. He found two more. Gray flint. Then he found a coin. Or a button. Deep crust of verdigris. He chipped at it with the nail of his thumb. It was a coin. He took out his knife and chiseled at it with care. The lettering was in spanish. He started to call to the boy where he trudged ahead and then he looked about at the gray country and the gray sky and he dropped the coin and hurried on to catch up.

They stood in front of the house looking at it. There was a gravel drive that curved away to the south. A brick loggia. Double stairs that swept up to the columned portico. At the rear of the house a brick dependency that may once have been a kitchen. Beyond that a log cabin. He started up the stairs but the boy pulled at his sleeve.

Can we wait a while?

Okay. But it's getting dark.

I know.

Okay.

They sat on the steps and looked out over the country.

There's no one here, the man said.

Okay.

Are you still scared?

Yes.

We're okay.

Okay.

. . .

They went up the stairs to the broad brickfloored porch. The door was painted black and it was propped open with a cinderblock. Dried leaves and weeds blown behind it. The boy clutched his hand. Why is the door open, Papa?

It just is. It's probably been open for years. Maybe the last people propped it open to carry their things out.

Maybe we should wait till tomorrow.

Come on. We'll take a quick look. Before it gets too dark. If we secure the area then maybe we can have a fire.

But we wont stay in the house will we?

We dont have to stay in the house.

Okay.

Let's have a drink of water.

Okay.

He took the bottle from the side pocket of his parka and screwed off the top and watched the boy drink. Then he took a drink himself and put the lid back on and took the boy's hand and they entered the darkened hall. High ceiling. An imported chandelier. At the landing on the stairs was a tall palladian window and the faintest shape of it headlong on the stairwell wall in the day's last light.

We dont have to go upstairs, do we? the boy whispered.

No. Maybe tomorrow.

After we've secured the area.

Yes.

Okay.

They entered the drawingroom. The shape of a carpet beneath the silty ash. Furniture shrouded in sheeting. Pale squares on the walls where paintings once had hung. In the room on the other side of the foyer stood a grand piano. Their own shapes sectioned in the thin and watery glass of the window there. They entered and stood listening. They wandered through the rooms like skeptical housebuyers. They stood looking out through the tall windows at the darkening land.

In the kitchen there was cutlery and cooking pans and english china. A butler's pantry where the door closed softly behind them. Tile floor and rows of shelves and on the shelves several dozen quart jars. He crossed the room and picked one up and blew the dust from it. Green beans. Slices of red pepper standing among the ordered rows. Tomatoes. Corn. New potatoes. Okra. The boy watched him. The man wiped the dust from the caps of the jars and pushed on the lids with his thumb. It was getting dark fast.

He carried a pair of the jars to the window and held them up and turned them. He looked at the boy. These may be poison, he said. We'll have to cook everything really well. Is that okay?

I dont know.

What do you want to do?

You have to say.

We both have to say.

Do you think they're okay?

I think if we cook them really good they'll be all right.

Okay. Why do you think nobody has eaten them?

I think nobody found them. You cant see the house from the road.

We saw it.

You saw it.

The boy studied the jars.

What do you think? the man said.

I think we've got no choice.

I think you're right. Let's get some wood before it gets any darker.

They carried armloads of dead limbs up the back stairs through the kitchen and into the diningroom and broke them to length and stuffed the fireplace full. He lit the fire and smoke curled up over the painted wooden lintel and rose to the ceiling and curled down again. He fanned the blaze with a magazine and soon the flue began to draw and the fire roared in the room lighting up the walls and the ceiling and the glass chandelier in its myraid facets. The flames lit the darkening glass of the window where the boy stood in hooded silhouette like a troll come in from the night. He seemed stunned by the heat. The man pulled the sheets off the long Empire table in the center of the room and shook them out and made a nest of them in front of the hearth. He sat the boy down and pulled off his shoes and pulled off the dirty rags with which his feet were wrapped. Everything's okay, he whispered. Everything's okay.

He found candles in a kitchen drawer and lit two of them and then melted wax onto the counter and stood them in the wax. He went outside and brought in more wood and piled it beside the hearth. The boy had not moved. There were pots and pans in the kitchen and he wiped one out and stood it on the counter and then he tried to open one of the jars but he could not. He carried a jar of green beans and one of potatoes to the front door and by the light of a candle standing in a glass he knelt and placed the first jar sideways in the space between the door and the jamb and pulled the door against it. Then he squatted in the foyer floor and hooked his foot over the outside edge of the door and pulled it against the lid and twisted the jar in his hands. The knurled lid turned in the wood grinding the paint. He took a fresh grip on the glass and pulled the door tighter and tried again. The lid slipped in the wood, then it held. He turned the jar slowly in his hands, then took it from the jamb and turned off the ring of the lid and set it in the floor. Then he opened the second jar and rose and carried them back into the kitchen, holding the glass in his other hand with the candle rolling about and sputtering. He tried to push the lids up off the jars with his thumbs but they were on too tight. He thought that was a good sign. He set the edge of the lid on the counter and punched the top of the jar with his fist and the lid snapped off and fell in the floor and he raised the jar and sniffed at it. It smelled delicious. He poured the potatoes and the beans into a pot and carried the pot into the diningroom and set it in the fire.

.   .   .

They ate slowly out of bone china bowls, sitting at opposite sides of the table with a single candle burning between them. The pistol lying to hand like another dining implement. The warming house creaked and groaned. Like a thing being called out of long hibernation. The boy nodded over his bowl and his spoon clattered to the floor. The man rose and came around and carried him to the hearth and put him down in the sheets and covered him with the blankets. He must have gone back to the table because he woke in the night lying there with his face in his crossed arms. It was cold in the room and outside the wind was blowing. The windows rattled softly in their frames. The candle had burned out and the fire was down to coals. He rose and built back the fire and sat beside the boy and pulled the blankets over him and brushed back his filthy hair. I think maybe they are watching, he said. They are watching for a thing that even death cannot undo and if they do not see it they will turn away from us and they will not come back.

The boy didnt want him to go upstairs. He tried to reason with him. There could be blankets up there, he said. We need to take a look.

I dont want you to go up there.

There's no one here.

There could be.

There's no one here. Dont you think they'd have come down by now?

Maybe they're scared.

I'll tell them we wont hurt them.

Maybe they're dead.

Then they wont mind if we take a few things. Look, whatever is up there it's better to know about it than to not know.

Why?

Why. Well, because we dont like surprises. Surprises are scary. And we dont like to be scared. And there could be things up there that we need. We have to take a look.

Okay.

Okay? Just like that?

Well. You're not going to listen to me.

I have been listening to you.

Not very hard.

There's no one here. There has been no one here for years. There are no tracks in the ash. Nothing disturbed. No furniture burned in the fireplace. There's food here.

Tracks dont stay in the ash. You said so yourself. The wind blows them away.

I'm going up.

They stayed at the house for four days eating and sleeping. He'd found more blankets upstairs and they dragged in great piles of wood and stacked the wood in the corner of the room to dry. He found an antique bucksaw of wood and wire that he used to saw the dead trees to length. The teeth were rusty and dull and he sat in front of the fire with a rattail file and tried to sharpen them but to little purpose. There was a creek some hundred yards from the house and he hauled endless pails of water across the stubble fields and the mud and they heated water and bathed in a tub off the back bedroom on the lower floor and he cut their hair and shaved his beard. They had clothes and blankets and pillows from the upstairs rooms and they fitted themselves out in new attire, the boy's trousers cut to length with his knife. He made a nesting place in front of the hearth, turning over a tallboy chest to use as a headboard for their bed and to hold the heat. All the while it continued to rain. He set pails under the downspouts at the housecorners to catch fresh water off the old standingseam metal roof and at night he could hear the rain drumming in the upper rooms and dripping through the house.

They rummaged through the outbuildings for anything of use. He found a wheelbarrow and pulled it out and tipped it over and turned the wheel slowly, examining the tire. The rubber was glazed and cracked but he thought it might hold air and he looked through old boxes and jumbles of tools and found a bicycle pump and screwed the end of the hose to the valvestem of the tire and began to pump. The air leaked out around the rim but he turned the wheel and had the boy hold down the tire until it caught and he got it pumped up. He unscrewed the hose and turned the wheel-barrow over and trundled it across the floor and back. Then he pushed it outside for the rain to clean. When they left two days later the weather had cleared and they set out down the muddy road pushing the wheelbarrow with their new blankets and the jars of canned goods wrapped in their extra clothes. He'd found a pair of workshoes and the boy was wearing blue tennis shoes with rags stuffed into the toes and they had fresh sheeting for face masks. When they got to the blacktop they had to turn back along the road to fetch the cart but it was less than a mile. The boy walked alongside with one hand on the wheelbarrow. We did good, didnt we Papa? he said. Yes we did.

They ate well but they were still a long way from the coast. He knew that he was placing hopes where he'd no reason to. He hoped it would be brighter where for all he knew the world grew darker daily. He'd once found a light-meter in a camera store that he thought he might use to average out readings for a few months and he carried it around with him for a long time thinking he might find some batteries for it but he never did. At night when he woke coughing he'd sit up with his hand pushed over his head against the blackness. Like a man waking in a grave. Like those disinterred dead from his childhood that had been relocated to accommodate a highway. Many had died in a cholera epidemic and they'd been buried in haste in wooden boxes and the boxes were rotting and falling open. The dead came to light lying on their sides with their legs drawn up and some lay on their stomachs. The dull green antique coppers spilled from out the tills of their eyesockets onto the stained and rotted coffin floors.

. . .

They stood in a grocery store in a small town where a mounted deerhead hung from the wall. The boy stood looking at it a long time. There was broken glass in the floor and the man made him wait at the door while he kicked through the trash in his workshoes but he found nothing. There were two gas pumps outside and they sat on the concrete apron and lowered a small tin can on a string into the underground tank and hauled it up and poured the cupful of gasoline it held into a plastic jug and lowered it again. They'd tied a small length of pipe to the can to sink it and they crouched over the tank like apes fishing with sticks in an anthill for the better part of an hour until the jug was full. Then they screwed on the cap and set the jug in the bottom rack of the cart and went on.

Long days. Open country with the ash blowing over the road. The boy sat by the fire at night with the pieces of the map across his knees. He had the names of towns and rivers by heart and he measured their progress daily.

They ate more sparingly. They'd almost nothing left. The boy stood in the road holding the map. They listened but they could hear nothing. Still he could see open country to the east and the air was different. Then they came upon it from a turn in the road and they stopped and stood with the salt wind blowing in their hair where they'd lowered the hoods of their coats to listen. Out there was the gray beach with the slow combers rolling dull and leaden and the distant sound of it. Like the desolation of some alien sea breaking on the shores of a world unheard of. Out on the tidal flats lay a tanker half careened. Beyond that the ocean vast and cold and shifting heavily like a slowly heaving vat of slag and then the gray squall line of ash. He looked at the boy. He could see the disappointment in his face. I'm sorry it's not blue, he said. That's okay, said the boy.

An hour later they were sitting on the beach and staring out at the wall of smog across the horizon. They sat with their heels dug into the sand and watched the bleak sea wash up at their feet. Cold. Desolate. Birdless. He'd left the cart in the bracken beyond the dunes and they'd taken blankets with them and sat wrapped in them in the wind-shade of a great driftwood log. They sat there for a long time. Along the shore of the cove below them windrows of small bones in the wrack. Further down the saltbleached ribcages of what may have been cattle. Gray salt rime on the rocks. The wind blew and dry seedpods scampered down the sands and stopped and then went on again.

Do you think there could be ships out there?
I dont think so.
They wouldnt be able to see very far.
No. They wouldnt.
What's on the other side?
Nothing.
There must be something.
Maybe there's a father and his little boy and they're sitting on the beach.
That would be okay.
Yes. That would be okay.
And they could be carrying the fire too?
They could be. Yes.
But we dont know.
We dont know.
So we have to be vigilant.
We have to be vigilant. Yes.
How long can we stay here?
I dont know. We dont have much to eat.

I know.

You like it.

Yeah.

Me too.

Can I go swimming?

Swimming?

Yes.

You'll freeze your tokus off.

I know.

It will be really cold. Worse than you think.

That's okay.

I dont want to have to come in after you.

You dont think I should go.

You can go.

But you dont think I should.

No. I think you should.

Really?

Yes. Really.

Okay.

He rose and let the blanket fall to the sand and then stripped out of his coat and out of his shoes and clothes. He stood naked, clutching himself and dancing. Then he went running down the beach. So white. Knobby spine-bones. The razorous shoulder blades sawing under the pale skin. Running naked and leaping and screaming into the slow roll of the surf.

By the time he came out he was blue with cold and his teeth were chattering. He walked down to meet him and wrapped him shuddering in the blanket and held him until he stopped gasping. But when he looked the boy was crying. What is it? he said. Nothing. No, tell me. Nothing. It's nothing.

With dark they built a fire against the log and ate plates of okra and beans and the last of the canned potatoes. The fruit was long gone. They drank tea and sat by the fire and they slept in the sand and listened to the roll of the surf in the bay. The long shudder and fall of it. He got up in the night and walked out and stood on the beach wrapped in his blankets. Too black to see. Taste of salt on his lips. Waiting. Waiting. Then the slow boom falling downshore. The seething hiss of it washing over the beach and drawing away again. He thought there could be deathships out

233

there yet, drifting with their lolling rags of sail. Or life in the deep. Great squid propelling themselves over the floor of the sea in the cold darkness. Shuttling past like trains, eyes the size of saucers. And perhaps beyond those shrouded swells another man did walk with another child on the dead gray sands. Slept but a sea apart on another beach among the bitter ashes of the world or stood in their rags lost to the same indifferent sun.

He remembered waking once on such a night to the clatter of crabs in the pan where he'd left steakbones from the night before. Faint deep coals of the driftwood fire pulsing in the onshore wind. Lying under such a myriad of stars. The sea's black horizon. He rose and walked out and stood barefoot in the sand and watched the pale surf appear all down the shore and roll and crash and darken again. When he went back to the fire he knelt and smoothed her hair as she slept and he said if he were God he would have made the world just so and no different.

When he got back the boy was awake and he was scared. He'd been calling out but not loud enough that he could hear him. The man put his arms around him. I couldnt hear you, he said. I couldnt hear you for the surf. He put wood on the fire and fanned it to life and they lay in their blankets watching the flames twist in the wind and then they slept.

In the morning he rekindled the fire and they ate and watched the shore. The cold and rainy look of it not so different from seascapes in the northern world. No gulls or shorebirds. Charred and senseless artifacts strewn down the shoreline or rolling in the surf. They gathered driftwood and stacked it and covered it with the tarp and then set off down the beach. We're beachcombers, he said.

What is that?

It's people who walk along the beach looking for things of value that might have washed up.

What kind of things?

Any kind of things. Anything that you might be able to use.

Do you think we'll find anything?

I dont know. We'll take a look.

Take a look, the boy said.

· · ·

They stood on the rock jetty and looked out to the south. A gray salt spittle lagging and curling in the rock pool. Long curve of beach beyond. Gray as lava sand. The wind coming off the water smelled faintly of iodine. That was all. There was no sea smell to it. On the rocks the remnants of some dark seamoss. They crossed and went on. At the end of the strand their way was blocked by a headland and they left the beach and took an old path up through the dunes and through the dead seaoats until they came out upon a low promontory. Below them a hook of land shrouded in the dark scud blowing down the shore and beyond that lying half over and awash the shape of a sailboat's hull. They crouched in the dry tufts of grass and watched. What should we do? the boy said.

Let's just watch for a while.

I'm cold.

I know. Let's move down a little ways. Out of the wind.

He sat holding the boy in front of him. The dead grass thrashed softly. Out there a gray desolation. The endless seacrawl. How long do we have to sit here? the boy said.

Not long.

Do you think there are people on the boat, Papa?

I dont think so.

They'd be all tilted over.

Yes they would. Can you see any tracks out there?

No.

Let's just wait a while.

I'm cold.

They trekked out along the crescent sweep of beach, keeping to the firmer sand below the tidewrack. They stood, their clothes flapping softly. Glass floats covered with a gray crust. The bones of seabirds. At the tide line a woven mat of weeds and the ribs of fishes in their millions stretching along the shore as far as eye could see like an isocline of death. One vast salt sepulchre. Senseless. Senseless.

From the end of the spit to the boat there was perhaps a hundred feet of open water. They stood looking at the boat. Some sixty feet long, stripped to the deck, keeled over in ten or twelve feet of water. It had been a twin-masted rig of some sort but the masts were broken off close to the deck and the only thing remaining topside were some brass cleats and a few of the rail stanchions along the edge of the deck. That and the steel hoop of the wheel sticking up out of the cockpit aft. He turned and studied the beach and the dunes beyond. Then he handed the boy the pistol and sat in the sand and began to unlace the cords of his shoes.

What are you going to do, Papa?

Take a look.

Can I go with you?

No. I want you to stay here.

I want to go with you.

You have to stand guard. And besides the water's deep.

Will I be able to see you?

Yes. I'll keep checking on you. To make sure everything's okay.

I want to go with you.

He stopped. You cant, he said. Our clothes would blow away. Somebody has to take care of things.

He folded everything into a pile. God it was cold. He bent and kissed the boy on his forehead. Stop worrying, he said. Just keep a lookout. He waded naked into the water and stood and laved himself wet. Then he trudged out splashing and dove headlong.

.   .   .

He swam the length of the steel hull and turned, treading water, gasping with the cold. Amidships the sheer-rail was just awash. He pulled himself along to the transom. The steel was gray and saltscoured but he could make out the worn gilt lettering. Pájaro de Esperanza. Tenerife. An empty pair of lifeboat davits. He got hold of the rail and pulled himself aboard and turned and crouched on the slant of the wood deck shivering. A few lengths of braided cable snapped off at the turnbuckles. Shredded holes in the wood where hardware had been ripped out. Some terrible force to sweep the decks of everything. He waved at the boy but he didnt wave back.

The cabin was low with a vaulted roof and portholes along the side. He crouched and wiped away the gray salt and looked in but he could see nothing. He tried the low teak door but it was locked. He gave it a shove with his bony shoulder. He looked around for something to pry with. He was shivering uncontrollably and his teeth were chattering. He thought about kicking the door with the flat of his foot but then he thought that was not a good idea. He held his elbow in his hand and banged into the door again. He felt it give. Very slightly. He kept at it. The jamb was splitting on the inside and it finally gave way and he pushed it open and stepped down the companionway into the cabin.

A stagnant bilge along the lower bulkhead filled with wet papers and trash. A sour smell over everything. Damp and clammy. He thought the boat had been ransacked but it was the sea that had done it. There was a mahogany table in the middle of the saloon with hinged fiddles. The locker doors hanging open into the room and all the brasswork a dull green. He went through to the forward cabins. Past the galley. Flour and coffee in the floor and canned goods half crushed and rusting. A head with a stainless steel toilet and sink. The weak sea light fell through the clerestory portholes. Gear scattered everywhere. A mae west floating in the seepage.

He was half expecting some horror but there was none. The mattress pads in the cabins had been slung into the floor and bedding and clothing were piled against the wall. Everything wet. A door stood open to the locker in the bow but it was too dark to see inside. He ducked his head and stepped in and felt about. Deep bins with hinged wooden covers. Sea gear piled in the floor. He began to drag everything out and pile it on the tilted bed. Blankets, foulweather gear. He came up with a damp sweater and pulled it over his head. He found a pair of yellow rubber seaboots and he found a nylon jacket and he zipped himself into that and pulled on the stiff yellow breeches from the souwester gear and thumbed the suspenders up over his shoulders and pulled on the boots. Then he went back up on the deck. The boy was sitting as he'd left him, watching the ship. He stood up in alarm and the man realized that in his new clothes he made an uncertain figure. It's me, he called, but the boy only stood there and he waved to him and went below again.

In the second stateroom there were drawers under the berth that were still in place and he lifted them free and slid them out. Manuals and papers in spanish. Bars of soap. A black leather valise covered in mold with papers inside. He put the soap in the pocket of his coat and stood. There were books in spanish strewn across the berth, swollen and shapeless. A single volume wedged in the rack against the forward bulkhead.

. . .

He found a rubberized canvas seabag and he prowled the rest of the ship in his boots, pushing himself off the bulkheads against the tilt, the yellow slicker pants rattling in the cold. He filled the bag with odds and ends of clothing. A pair of women's sneakers he thought would fit the boy. A foldingknife with a wooden handle. A pair of sunglasses. Still there was something perverse in his searching. Like exhausting the least likely places first when looking for something lost. Finally he went into the galley. He turned on the stove and turned it off again.

He unlatched and raised the hatch to the engine compartment. Half flooded and pitch dark. No smell of gas or oil. He closed it again. There were lockers built into the benches in the cockpit that held cushions, sailcanvas, fishing gear. In a locker behind the wheel pedestal he found coils of nylon rope and steel bottles of gas and a toolbox made of fiberglass. He sat in the floor of the cockpit and sorted through the tools. Rusty but serviceable. Pliers, screwdrivers, wrenches. He latched the toolbox shut and stood and looked for the boy. He was huddled in the sand asleep with his head on the pile of clothes.

. . .

He carried the toolbox and one of the bottles of gas into the galley and went forward and made a last tour of the staterooms. Then he set about going through the lockers in the saloon, looking through folders and papers in plastic boxes, trying to find the ship's log. He found a set of china packed away unused in a wooden crate filled with excelsior. Most of it broken. Service for eight, carrying the name of the ship. A gift, he thought. He lifted out a teacup and turned it in his palm and put it back. The last thing he found was a square oak box with dovetailed corners and a brass plate let into the lid. He thought it might be a humidor but it was the wrong shape and when he picked it up and felt the weight of it he knew what it was. He unsnapped the corroding latches and opened it. Inside was a brass sextant, possibly a hundred years old. He lifted it from the fitted case and held it in his hand. Struck by the beauty of it. The brass was dull and there were patches of green on it that took the form of another hand that once had held it but otherwise it was perfect. He wiped the verdigris from the plate at the base. Hezzaninth, London. He held it to his eye and turned the wheel. It was the first thing he'd seen in a long time that stirred him. He held it in his hand and then he fitted it back into the blue baize lining of the case and closed the lid and snapped the latches shut and set it back in the locker and closed the door.

When he went back up on deck again to look for the boy the boy was not there. A moment of panic before he saw him walking along the bench downshore with the pistol hanging in his hand, his head down. Standing there he felt the hull of the ship lift and slide. Just slightly. Tide coming in. Slapping along the rocks of the jetty down there. He turned and went back down into the cabin.

He'd brought the two coils of rope from the locker and he measured the diameter of them with the span of his hand and that by three and then counted the number of coils. Fifty foot ropes. He hung them over a cleat on the gray teakwood deck and went back down into the cabin. He collected everything and stacked it against the table. There were some plastic jugs of water in the locker off the galley but all were empty save one. He picked up one of the empties and saw that the plastic had cracked and the water leaked out and he guessed they had frozen somewhere on the ship's aimless voyagings. Probably several times.

He took the half full jug and set it on the table and unscrewed the cap and sniffed the water and then raised the jug in both hands and drank. Then he drank again.

The cans in the galley floor did not look in any way salvable and even in the locker there were some that were badly rusted and some that wore an ominous bulbed look. They'd all been stripped of their labels and the contents written on the metal in black marker pen in spanish. Not all of which he knew. He sorted through them, shaking them, squeezing them in his hand. He stacked them on the counter above the small galley refrigerator. He thought there must be crates of foodstuffs packed somewhere in the hold but he didnt think any of it would be edible. In any case there was a limit to what they could take in the cart. It occurred to him that he took this windfall in a fashion dangerously close to matter of fact but still he said what he had said before. That good luck might be no such thing. There were few nights lying in the dark that he did not envy the dead.

He found a can of olive oil and some cans of milk. Tea in a rusted metal caddy. A plastic container of some sort of meal that he did not recognize. A half empty can of coffee. He went methodically through the shelves in the locker, sorting what to take from what to leave. When he had carried everything into the saloon and stacked it against the companionway he went back into the galley and opened the toolbox and set about removing one of the burners from the little gimballed stove. He disconnected the braided flexline and removed the aluminum spiders from the burners and put one of them in the pocket of his coat. He unfastened the brass fittings with a wrench and took the burners loose. Then he uncoupled them and fastened the hose to the coupling pipe and fitted the other end of the hose to the gasbottle and carried it out to the saloon. Lastly he made a bindle in a plastic tarp of some cans of juice and cans of fruit and of vegetables and tied it with a cord and then he stripped out of his clothes and piled them among the goods he'd collected and went up onto the deck naked and slid down to the railing with the tarp and swung over the side and dropped into the gray and freezing sea.

He waded ashore in the last of the light and swung the tarp down and palmed the water off his arms and chest and went to get his clothes. The boy followed him. He kept asking him about his shoulder, blue and discolored from where he'd slammed it against the hatch door. It's all right, the man said. It doesnt hurt. We got lots of stuff. Wait till you see.

They hurried down the beach against the light. What if the boat washes away? the boy said.

It wont wash away.

It could.

No it wont. Come on. Are you hungry?

Yes.

We're going to eat well tonight. But we need to get a move on.

I'm hurrying, Papa.

And it may rain.

How can you tell?

I can smell it.

What does it smell like?

Wet ashes. Come on.

Then he stopped. Where's the pistol? he said.

The boy froze. He looked terrified.

Christ, the man said. He looked back up the beach.

They were already out of sight of the boat. He looked at the boy. The boy had put his hands on top of this head and he was about to cry. I'm sorry, he said. I'm really sorry.

He set down the tarp with the canned goods. We have to go back.

I'm sorry, Papa.

It's okay. It will still be there.

The boy stood with his shoulders slumped. He was beginning to sob. The man knelt and put his arms around him. It's all right, he said. I'm the one who's supposed to make sure we have the pistol and I didnt do it. I forgot.

I'm sorry, Papa.

Come on. We're okay. Everything's okay.

The pistol was where he'd left it in the sand. The man picked it up and shook it and he sat and pulled the cylinder pin and handed it to the boy. Hold this, he said.

Is it okay, Papa?

Of course it's okay.

He rolled the cylinder out into his hand and blew the sand from it and handed it to the boy and he blew through the barrel and he blew the sand out of the frame and then took the parts from the boy and refitted everything and cocked the pistol and lowered the hammer and cocked it again. He aligned the cylinder for the true cartridge to come up and he let the hammer down and put the pistol in his parka and stood up. We're okay, he said. Come on.

Is the dark going to catch us?

I dont know.

It is, isnt it?

Come on. We'll hurry.

The dark did catch them. By the time they reached the headland path it was too dark to see anything. They stood in the wind from off the sea with the grass hissing all about them, the boy holding on to his hand. We just have to keep going, the man said. Come on.

I cant see.

I know. We'll just take it one step at a time.

Okay.

Dont let go.

Okay.

No matter what.

No matter what.

. . .

They went on in the perfect blackness, sightless as the blind. He held out one hand before him although there was nothing on that salt heath to collide with. The surf sounded more distant but he took his bearings by the wind as well and after tottering on for the better part of an hour they emerged from the grass and seaoats and stood again on the dry sand of the upper beach. The wind was colder. He'd brought the boy around on the lee side of him when suddenly the beach before them appeared shuddering out of the blackness and vanished again.

What was that, Papa?

It's okay. It's lightning. Come on.

He slung the tarp of goods up over his shoulder and took the boy's hand and they went on, tramping in the sand like parade horses against tripping over some piece of driftwood or seawrack. The weird gray light broke over the beach again. Far away a faint rumble of thunder muffled in the murk. I think I saw our tracks, he said.

So we're going the right way.

Yes. The right way.

I'm really cold, Papa.

I know. Pray for lightning.

·   ·   ·

They went on. When the light broke over the beach again he saw that the boy was bent over and was whispering to himself. He looked for their tracks going up the beach but he could not see them. The wind had picked up even more and he was waiting for the first spits of rain. If they got caught out on the beach in a rainstorm in the night they would be in trouble. They turned their faces away from the wind, holding on to the hoods of their parkas. The sand rattling against their legs and racing away in the dark and the thunder cracking just offshore. The rain came in off the sea hard and slant and stung their faces and he pulled the boy against him.

They stood in the downpour. How far had they come? He waited for the lightning but it was tailing off and when the next one came and then the next he knew that the storm had taken out their tracks. They trudged on through the sand at the upper edge of the beach, hoping to see the shape of the log where they'd camped. Soon the lightning was all but gone. Then in a shift in the wind he heard a distant faint patter. He stopped. Listen, he said.

What is it?

Listen.

I dont hear anything.

Come on.

What is it, Papa?

It's the tarp. It's the rain falling on the tarp.

They went on, stumbling through the sand and the trash along the tideline. They came upon the tarp almost at once and he knelt and dropped the bindle and groped about for the rocks he'd weighed the plastic with and pushed them beneath it. He raised up the tarp and pulled it over them and then used the rocks to hold down the edges inside. He got the boy out of his wet coat and pulled the blankets over them, the rain pelting them through the plastic. He shucked off his own coat and held the boy close and soon they were asleep.

In the night the rain ceased and he woke and lay listening. The heavy wash and thud of the surf after the wind had died. In the first dull light he rose and walked down the beach. The storm had littered the shore and he walked the tideline looking for anything of use. In the shallows beyond the breakwater an ancient corpse rising and falling among the driftwood. He wished he could hide it from the boy but the boy was right. What was there to hide? When he got back he was awake sitting in the sand watching him. He was wrapped in the blankets and he'd spread their wet coats over the dead weeds to dry. He walked up and eased himself down beside him and they sat watching the leaden sea lift and fall beyond the breakers.

They were most of the morning offloading the ship. He kept a fire going and he'd wade ashore naked and shivering and drop the towrope and stand in the warmth of the blaze while the boy towed in the seabag through the slack swells and dragged it onto the beach. They emptied out the bag and spread blankets and clothing out on the warm sand to dry before the fire. There was more on the boat than they could carry and he thought they might stay a few days on the beach and eat as much as they could but it was dangerous. They slept that night in the sand with the fire standing off the cold and their goods scattered all about them. He woke coughing and rose and took a drink of water and dragged more wood onto the fire, whole logs of it that sent up a great cascade of sparks. The salt wood burned orange and blue in the fire's heart and he sat watching it a long time. Later he walked up the beach, his long shadow reaching over the sands before him, sawing about with the wind in the fire. Coughing. Coughing. He bent over, holding his knees. Taste of blood. The slow surf crawled and seethed in the dark and he thought about his life but there was no life to think about and after a while he walked back. He got a can of peaches from the bag and opened it and sat before the fire and ate the peaches slowly with his spoon while the boy slept. The fire flared in the wind and sparks raced away down the sand. He set the empty tin between his feet. Every day is a lie, he said. But you are dying. That is not a lie.

They carried their new stores bundled in tarps or blankets down the beach and packed everything into the cart. The boy tried to carry too much and when they stopped to rest he'd take part of his load and put it with his own. The boat had shifted slightly in the storm. He stood looking at it. The boy watched him. Are you going back out there? he said.

I think so. One last look around.

I'm kind of scared.

We're okay. Just keep watch.

We've got more than we can carry now.

I know. I just want to take a look.

Okay.

He went over the ship from bow to stern again. Stop. Think. He sat in the floor of the saloon with his feet in the rubber boots propped against the pedestal of the table. It was already getting dark. He tried to remember what he knew about boats. He got up and went out on deck again. The boy was sitting by the fire. He stepped down into the cockpit and sat on the bench with his back against the bulkhead, his feet on the deck almost at eye level. He had on nothing but the sweater and the souwester outfit over that but there was little warmth to it and he could not stop shivering. He was about to get up again when he realized that he'd been looking at the fasteners in the bulkhead on the far side of the cockpit. There were four of them. Stainless steel. At one time the benches had been covered with cushions and he could see the ties at the corner where they'd ripped away. At the bottom center of the bulkhead just above the seat there was a nylon strap sticking out, the end of it doubled and cross-stitched. He looked at the fasteners again. They were rotary latches with wings for your thumb. He got up and knelt at the bench and turned each one all the way to the left. They were springloaded and when he had them undone he took hold of the strap at the bottom of the board and pulled it and the board slid down and came free. Inside under the deck was a space that held some rolled sails and what looked to be a two man rubber raft rolled and tied with bungee cords. A pair of small plastic oars. A box of flares. And behind that was a composite toolbox, the opening of the lid sealed with black electrical tape. He pulled it free and found the end of the tape and peeled it off all the way around and unlatched the chrome snaps and opened the box. Inside was a yellow plastic flashlight, an electric strobebeacon powered by a drycell, a first-aid kit. A yellow plastic EPIRB. And a black plastic case about the size of a book. He lifted it out and unsnapped the latches and opened it. Inside was fitted an old 37 millimeter bronze flarepistol. He lifted it from the case in both hands and turned it and looked at it. He depressed the lever and broke it open. The chamber was empty but there were eight rounds of flares fitted in a plastic container, short and squat and newlooking. He fitted the pistol back in the case and closed and latched the lid.

.   .   .

He waded ashore shivering and coughing and wrapped himself in a blanket and sat in the warm sand in front of the fire with the boxes beside him. The boy crouched and tried to put his arms around him which at least brought a smile. What did you find, Papa? he said.

I found a first-aid kit. And I found a flarepistol.

What's that?

I'll show you. It's to signal with.

Is that what you went to look for?

Yes.

How did you know it was there?

Well, I was hoping it was there. It was mostly luck.

He opened the case and turned it for the boy to see.

It's a gun.

A flaregun. It shoots a thing up in the air and it makes a big light.

Can I look at it?

Sure you can.

The boy lifted the gun from the case and held it. Can you shoot somebody with it? he said.

You could.

Would it kill them?

No. But it might set them on fire.

Is that why you got it?

Yes.

Because there's nobody to signal to. Is there?

No.

I'd like to see it.

You mean shoot it?

Yes.

We can shoot it.

For real?

Sure.

In the dark?

Yes. In the dark.

It could be like a celebration.

Like a celebration. Yes.

Can we shoot it tonight?

Why not?

Is it loaded?

No. But we can load it.

The boy stood holding the gun. He pointed it toward the sea. Wow, he said.

He got dressed and they set out down the beach carrying the last of their plunder. Where do you think the people went, Papa?

That were on the ship?

Yes.

I dont know.

Do you think they died?

I dont know.

But the odds are not in their favor.

The man smiled. The odds are not in their favor?

No. Are they?

No. Probably not.

I think they died.

Maybe they did.

I think that's what happened to them.

They could be alive somewhere, the man said. It's possible. The boy didnt answer. They went on. They'd wrapped their feet in sailcloth and bound them up in blue plastic pampooties cut from a tarp and they left strange tracks in their comings and going. He thought about the boy and his concerns and after a while he said: You're probably right. I think they're probably dead.

Because if they were alive we'd be taking their stuff.

And we're not taking their stuff.

I know.

Okay.

So how many people do you think are alive?

In the world?

In the world. Yes.

I dont know. Let's stop and rest.

Okay.

You're wearing me out.

Okay.

They sat among their bundles.

How long can we stay here, Papa?

You asked me that.

I know.

We'll see.

That means not very long.

Probably.

The boy poked holes in the sand with his fingers until he had a circle of them. The man watched him. I dont know how many people there are, he said. I dont think there are very many.

I know. He pulled his blanket about his shoulders and looked out down the gray and barren beach.

What is it? the man said.

Nothing.

No. Tell me.

There could be people alive someplace else.

Whereplace else?

I dont know. Anywhere.

You mean besides on earth?

Yes.

I dont think so. They couldnt live anyplace else.

Not even if they could get there?

No.

The boy looked away.

What? the man said.

He shook his head. I dont know what we're doing, he said.

The man started to answer. But he didnt. After a while he said: There are people. There are people and we'll find them. You'll see.

He fixed dinner while the boy played in the sand. He had a spatula made from a flattened foodtin and with it he built a small village. He dredged a grid of streets. The man walked down and squatted and looked at it. The boy looked up. The ocean's going to get it, isnt it? he said.

Yes.

That's okay.

Can you write the alphabet?

I can write it.

We dont work on your lessons any more.

I know.

Can you write something in the sand?

Maybe we could write a letter to the good guys. So if they came along they'd know we were here. We could write it up there where it wouldnt get washed away.

What if the bad guys saw it?

Yeah.

I shouldnt have said that. We could write them a letter.

The boy shook his head. That's okay, he said.

He loaded the flarepistol and as soon as it was dark they walked out down the beach away from the fire and he asked the boy if he wanted to shoot it.

You shoot it, Papa. You know how to do it.

Okay.

He cocked the gun and aimed it out over the bay and pulled the trigger. The flare arced up into the murk with a long whoosh and broke somewhere out over the water in a clouded light and hung there. The hot tendrils of magnesium drifted slowly down the dark and the pale foreshore tide started in the glare and slowly faded. He looked down at the boy's upturned face.

They couldnt see it very far, could they, Papa?

Who?

Anybody.

No. Not far.

If you wanted to show where you were.

You mean like to the good guys?

Yes. Or anybody that you wanted them to know where you were.

Like who?

I dont know.

Like God?

Yeah. Maybe somebody like that.

In the morning he built a fire and walked out on the beach while the boy slept. He was not gone long but he felt a strange unease and when he got back the boy was standing on the beach wrapped in his blankets waiting for him. He hurried his steps. By the time he got to him he was sitting down.

What is it? he said. What is it?

I dont feel good, Papa.

He cupped the boy's forehead in his hand. He was burning. He picked him up and carried him to the fire. It's okay, he said. You're going to be okay.

I think I'm going to be sick.

It's okay.

He sat with him in the sand and held his forehead while he bent and vomited. He wiped the boy's mouth with his hand. I'm sorry, the boy said. Shh. You didnt do anything wrong.

He carried him up to the camp and covered him with blankets. He tried to get him to drink some water. He put more wood on the fire and knelt with his hand on his forehead. You'll be all right he said. He was terrified.

Dont go away, the boy said.

Of course I wont go away.

Even for just a little while.

No. I'm right here.

Okay. Okay, Papa.

.   .   .

264

He held him all night, dozing off and waking in terror, feeling for the boy's heart. In the morning he was no better. He tried to get him to drink some juice but he would not. He pressed his hand to his forehead, conjuring up a coolness that would not come. He wiped his white mouth while he slept. I will do what I promised, he whispered. No matter what. I will not send you into the darkness alone.

He went through the first-aid kit from the boat but there was nothing much there of use. Aspirin. Bandages and disinfectant. Some antibiotics but they had a short shelflife. Still that was all he had and he helped the boy drink and put one of the capsules on his tongue. He was soaked in sweat. He'd already stripped him out of the blankets and now he unzipped him out of his coat and then out of his clothes and moved him away from the fire. The boy looked up at him. I'm so cold, he said.

I know. But you have a really high temperature and we have to get you cooled off.

Can I have another blanket?

Yes. Of course.

You wont go away.

No. I wont go away.

He carried the boy's filthy clothes into the surf and washed them, standing shivering in the cold salt water naked from the waist down and sloshing them up and down and wringing them out. He spread them by the fire on sticks angled into the sand and piled on more wood and went and sat by the boy again, smoothing his matted hair. In the evening he opened a can of soup and set it in the coals and he ate and watched the darkness come up. When he woke he was lying shivering in the sand and the fire had died almost to ash and it was black night. He sat up wildly and reached for the boy. Yes, he whispered. Yes.

He rekindled the fire and he got a cloth and wet it and put it over the boy's forehead. The wintry dawn was coming and when it was light enough to see he went into the woods beyond the dunes and came back dragging a great travois of dead limbs and branches and set about breaking them up and stacking them near the fire. He crushed aspirins in a cup and dissolved them in water and put in some sugar and sat and lifted the boy's head and held the cup while he drank.

He walked the beach, slumped and coughing. He stood looking out at the dark swells. He was staggering with fatigue. He went back and sat by the boy and refolded the cloth and wiped his face and then spread the cloth over his forehead. You have to stay near, he said. You have to be quick. So you can be with him. Hold him close. Last day of the earth.

The boy slept all day. He kept waking him up to drink the sugarwater, the boy's dry throat jerking and chugging. You have to drink he said. Okay, wheezed the boy. He twisted the cup into the sand beside him and cushioned the folded blanket under his sweaty head and covered him. Are you cold? he said. But the boy was already asleep.

He tried to stay awake all night but he could not. He woke endlessly and sat and slapped himself or rose to put wood on the fire. He held the boy and bent to hear the labored suck of air. His hand on the thin and laddered ribs. He walked out on the beach to the edge of the light and stood with his clenched fists on top of his skull and fell to his knees sobbing in rage.

It rained briefly in the night, a light patter on the tarp. He pulled it over them and turned and lay holding the child, watching the blue flames through the plastic. He fell into a dreamless sleep.

When he woke again he hardly knew where he was. The fire had died, the rain had ceased. He threw back the tarp and pushed himself up on his elbows. Gray daylight. The boy was watching him. Papa, he said.

Yes. I'm right here.

Can I have a drink of water?

Yes. Yes, of course you can. How are you feeling?

I feel kind of weird.

Are you hungry?

I'm just really thirsty.

Let me get the water.

He pushed back the blankets and rose and walked out past the dead fire and got the boy's cup and filled it out of the plastic water jug and came back and knelt and held the cup for him. You're going to be okay, he said. The boy drank. He nodded and looked at his father. Then he drank the rest of the water. More, he said.

He built a fire and propped the boy's wet clothes up and brought him a can of apple juice. Do you remember anything? he said.

About what?

About being sick.

I remember shooting the flaregun.

Do you remember getting the stuff from the boat?

He sat sipping the juice. He looked up. I'm not a retard, he said.

I know.

I had some weird dreams.

What about?

I dont want to tell you.

That's okay. I want you to brush your teeth.

With real toothpaste.

Yes.

Okay.

He checked all the foodtins but he could find nothing suspect. He threw out a few that looked pretty rusty. They sat that evening by the fire and the boy drank hot soup and the man turned his steaming clothes on the sticks and sat watching him until the boy became embarrassed. Stop watching me, Papa, he said.

Okay.

But he didnt.

In two days' time they were walking the beach as far as the headland and back, trudging along in their plastic bootees. They ate huge meals and he put up a sailcloth leanto with ropes and poles against the wind. They pruned down their stores to a manageable load for the cart and he thought they might leave in two more days. Then coming back to the camp late in the day he saw bootprints in the sand. He stopped and stood looking down the beach. Oh Christ, he said. Oh Christ.

What is it, Papa?

He pulled the pistol from his belt. Come on he said. Hurry.

The tarp was gone. Their blankets. The waterbottle and their campsite store of food. The sailcloth was blown up into the dunes. Their shoes were gone. He ran up through the swale of seaoats where he'd left the cart but the cart was gone. Everything. You stupid ass, he said. You stupid ass.

The boy was standing there wide-eyed. What happened, Papa?

They took everything. Come on.

The boy looked up. He was beginning to cry.

Stay with me, the man said. Stay right with me.

He could see the tracks of the cart where they sloughed up through the loose sand. Bootprints. How many? He lost the track on the better ground beyond the bracken and then picked it up again. When they got to the road he stopped the boy with his hand. The road was exposed to the wind from the sea and it was blown free of ash save for patches here and there. Dont step in the road, he said.

And stop crying. We need to get all the sand off of our feet. Here. Sit down.

He untied the wrappings and shook them out and tied them back again. I want you to help, he said. We're looking for sand. Sand in the road. Even just a little bit. To see which way they went. Okay?

Okay.

They set off down the blacktop in opposite directions. He'd not gone far before the boy called out. Here it is, Papa. They went this way. When he got there the boy was crouched in the road. Right here, he said. It was a half teaspoon of beachsand tilted from somewhere in the understructure of the grocery cart. The man stood and looked out down the road. Good work, he said. Let's go.

They set off at a jogtrot. A pace he thought he'd be able to keep up but he couldnt. He had to stop, leaning over and coughing. He looked up at the boy, wheezing. We'll have to walk, he said. If they hear us they'll hide by the side of the road. Come on.

How many are there, Papa?

I dont know. Maybe just one.

Are we going to kill them?

I dont know.

They went on. It was already late in the day and it was another hour and deep into the long dusk before they overtook the thief, bent over the loaded cart, trundling down the road before them. When he looked back and saw them he tried to run with the cart but it was useless and finally he stopped and stood behind the cart holding a butcher knife. When he saw the pistol he stepped back but he didnt drop the knife.

Get away from the cart, the man said.

He looked at them. He looked at the boy. He was an outcast from one of the communes and the fingers of his right hand had been cut away. He tried to hide it behind him. A sort of fleshy spatula. The cart was piled high. He'd taken everything.

Get away from the cart and put down the knife.

He looked around. As if there might be help somewhere. Scrawny, sullen, bearded, filthy. His old plastic coat held together with tape. The pistol was a double action but the man cocked it anyway. Two loud clicks. Otherwise only their breathing in the silence of the salt moorland. They could smell him in his stinking rags. If you dont put down the knife and get away from the cart, the man said, I'm going to blow your brains out. The thief looked at the child and what he saw was very sobering to him. He laid the knife on top of the blankets and backed away and stood.

Back. More.

He stepped back again.

Papa? the boy said.

Be quiet.

He kept his eyes on the thief. Goddamn you, he said.

Papa please dont kill the man.

The thief's eyes swung wildly. The boy was crying.

Come on, man. I done what you said. Listen to the boy.

Take your clothes off.

What?

Take them off. Every goddamned stitch.

Come on. Dont do this.

I'll kill you where you stand.

Dont do this, man.

I wont tell you again.

All right. All right. Just take it easy.

He stripped slowly and piled his vile rags in the road.

The shoes.

Come on, man.

The shoes.

The thief looked at the boy. The boy had turned away and put his hands over his ears. Okay, he said. Okay. He sat naked in the road and began to unlace the rotting pieces of leather laced to his feet. Then he stood up, holding them in one hand.

Put them in the cart.

He stepped forward and placed the shoes on top of the blankets and stepped back. Standing there raw and naked, filthy, starving. Covering himself with his hand. He was already shivering.

Put the clothes in.

He bent and scooped up the rags in his arms and piled them on top of the shoes. He stood there holding himself. Dont do this, man.

You didnt mind doing it to us.

I'm begging you.

Papa, the boy said.

Come on. Listen to the kid.

You tried to kill us.

I'm starving, man. You'd have done the same.

You took everything.

Come on, man. I'll die.

I'm going to leave you the way you left us.

Come on. I'm begging you.

He pulled the cart back and swung it around and put the pistol on top and looked at the boy. Let's go, he said. And they set out along the road south, with the boy crying and looking back at the nude and slatlike creature standing there in the road shivering and hugging himself. Oh Papa, he sobbed.

Stop it.

I cant stop it.

What do you think would have happened to us if we hadnt caught him? Just stop it.

I'm trying.

When they got to the curve in the road the man was still standing there. There was no place for him to go. The boy kept looking back and when he could no longer see him he stopped and then he just sat down in the road sobbing. The man pulled up and stood looking at him. He dug their shoes out of the cart and sat down and began to take the wrappings off the boy's feet. You have to stop crying, he said.

I cant.

He put on their shoes and then stood and walked back up the road but he couldnt see the thief. He came back and stood over the boy. He's gone, he said. Come on.

He's not gone, the boy said. He looked up. His face streaked with soot. He's not.

What do you want to do?

Just help him, Papa. Just help him.

The man looked back up the road.

He was just hungry, Papa. He's going to die.

He's going to die anyway.

He's so scared, Papa.

The man squatted and looked at him. I'm scared, he said. Do you understand? I'm scared.

The boy didnt answer. He just sat there with his head bowed, sobbing.

You're not the one who has to worry about everything.

The boy said something but he couldnt understand him. What? he said.

He looked up, his wet and grimy face. Yes I am, he said. I am the one.

. . .

They wheeled the tottering cart back up the road and stood there in the cold and the gathering dark and called but no one came.

He's afraid to answer, Papa.

Is this where we stopped?

I dont know. I think so.

They went up the road calling out in the empty dusk, their voices lost over the darkening shorelands. They stopped and stood with their hands cupped to their mouths, hallooing mindlessly into the waste. Finally he piled the man's shoes and clothes in the road. He put a rock on top of them. We have to go, he said. We have to go.

They made a dry camp with no fire. He sorted out cans for their supper and warmed them over the gas burner and they ate and the boy said nothing. The man tried to see his face in the blue light from the burner. I wasnt going to kill him, he said. But the boy didnt answer. They rolled themselves in the blankets and lay there in the dark. He thought he could hear the sea but perhaps it was just the wind. He could tell by his breathing that the boy was awake and after a while the boy said: But we did kill him.

· · ·

In the morning they ate and set out. The cart was so loaded it was hard to push and one of the wheels was giving out. The road bent its way along the coast, dead sheaves of saltgrass overhanging the pavement. The leadcolored sea shifting in the distance. The silence. He woke that night with the dull carbon light of the crossing moon beyond the murk making the shapes of the trees almost visible and he turned away coughing. Smell of rain out there. The boy was awake. You have to talk to me, he said.

I'm trying.

I'm sorry I woke you.

It's okay.

He got up and walked out to the road. The black shape of it running from dark to dark. Then a distant low rumble. Not thunder. You could feel it under your feet. A sound without cognate and so without description. Something imponderable shifting out there in the dark. The earth itself contracting with the cold. It did not come again. What time of year? What age the child? He walked out into the road and stood. The silence. The salitter drying from the earth. The mudstained shapes of flooded cities burned to the waterline. At a crossroads a ground set with dolmen stones where the spoken bones of oracles lay moldering. No sound but the wind. What will you say? A living man spoke these lines? He sharpened a quill with his small pen knife to scribe these things in sloe or lampblack? At some reckonable and entabled moment? He is coming to steal my eyes. To seal my mouth with dirt.

He went through the cans again one by one, holding them in his hand and squeezing them like a man checking for ripeness at a fruitstand. He sorted out two he thought questionable and packed away the rest and packed the cart and they set out upon the road again. In three days they came to a small port town and they hid the cart in a garage behind a house and piled old boxes over it and then sat in the house to see if anyone would come. No one did. He looked through the cabinets but there was nothing there. He needed vitamin D for the boy or he was going to get rickets. He stood at the sink and looked out down the driveway. Light the color of washwater congealing in the dirty panes of glass. The boy sat slumped at the table with his head in his arms.

They walked through the town and down to the docks. They saw no one. He had the pistol in the pocket of his coat and he carried the flaregun in his hand. They walked out on the pier, the rough boards dark with tar and fastened down with spikes to the timbers underneath. Wooden bollards. Faint smell of salt and creosote coming in off the bay. On the far shore a row of warehouses and the shape of a tanker red with rust. A tall gantry crane against the sullen sky. There's no one here, he said. The boy didnt answer.

They wheeled the cart through the back streets and across the railroad tracks and came into the main road again at the far edge of the town. As they passed the last of the sad wooden buildings something whistled past his head and clattered off the street and broke up against the wall of the block building on the other side. He grabbed the boy and fell on top of him and grabbed the cart to pull it to them. It tipped and fell over spilling the tarp and blankets into the street. In an upper window of the house he could see a man drawing a bow on them and he pushed the boy's head down and tried to cover him with his body. He heard the dull thwang of the bowstring and felt a sharp hot pain in his leg. Oh you bastard, he said. You bastard. He clawed the blankets to one side and lunged and grabbed the flaregun and raised up and cocked it and rested his arm on the side of the cart. The boy was clinging to him. When the man stepped back into the frame of the window to draw the bow again he fired. The flare went rocketing up toward the window in a long white arc and then they could hear the man screaming. He grabbed the boy and pushed him down and dragged the blankets over the top of him. Dont move, he said. Dont move and dont look. He pulled the blankets out into the street looking for the case for the flarepistol. It finally slid out of the cart and he snatched it up and opened it and took out the shells and reloaded the pistol and breeched it shut and put the rest of the loads in his pocket. Stay just like you are, he whispered. He patted the boy through the blankets and rose and ran limping across the street.

He entered the house through the back door with the flaregun leveled at his waist. The house was stripped out to the wall studs. He stepped through into the livingroom and stood at the stair landing. He listened for movement in the upper rooms. He looked out the front window to where the cart lay in the street and then he went up the stairs.

. . .

A woman was sitting in the corner holding the man. She'd taken off her coat to cover him. As soon as she saw him she began to curse him. The flare had burned out in the floor leaving a patch of white ash and there was a faint smell of burnt wood in the room. He crossed the room and looked out the window. The woman's eyes followed him. Scrawny, lank gray hair.

Who else is up here?

She didnt answer. He stepped past her and went through the rooms. His leg was bleeding badly. He could feel his trousers sticking to the skin. He went back into the front room. Where's the bow? he said.

I dont have it.

Where is it?

I dont know.

They left you here, didnt they?

I left myself here.

He turned and went limping down the stairs and he opened the front door and went out into the street backward watching the house. When he got to the cart he pulled it upright and piled their things back in. Stay close, he whispered. Stay close.

.   .   .

They put up in a store building at the end of the town. He wheeled the cart through and into a room at the rear and shut the door and pushed the cart against it sideways. He dug out the burner and the tank of gas and lit the burner and set it in the floor and then he unbuckled his belt and took off the bloodstained trousers. The boy watched. The arrow had cut a gash just above his knee about three inches long. It was still bleeding and his whole upper leg was discolored and he could see that the cut was deep. Some homemade broadhead beaten out of strapiron, an old spoon, God knows what. He looked at the boy. See if you can find the first-aid kit, he said.

The boy didnt move.

Get the first-aid kit, damn it. Dont just sit there.

He jumped up and went to the door and began digging under the tarp and the blankets piled in the cart. He came back with the kit and gave it to the man and the man took it without comment and set it in the concrete floor in front of him and unsnapped the catches and opened it. He reached and turned up the burner for the light. Bring me the water bottle, he said. The boy brought the bottle and the man unscrewed the lid and poured water over the wound and held it shut between his fingers while he wiped away the blood. He swabbed the wound with disinfectant and opened a plastic envelope with his teeth and took out a small hooked suture needle and a coil of silk thread and sat holding the silk to the light while he threaded it through the needle's eye. He took a clamp from the kit and caught the needle in the jaws and locked them and set about suturing the wound. He worked quickly and he took no great pains about it. The boy was crouching in the floor. He looked at him and he bent to the sutures again. You dont have to watch, he said.

Is it okay?

Yeah. It's okay.

Does it hurt?

Yes. It hurts.

He ran the knot down the thread and pulled it taut and cut off the silk with the scissors from the kit and looked at the boy. The boy was looking at what he'd done.

I'm sorry I yelled at you.

He looked up. That's okay, Papa.

Let's start over.

Okay.

. . .

In the morning it was raining and a hard wind was rattling the glass at the rear of the building. He stood looking out. A steel dock half collapsed and submerged in the bay. The wheelhouses of sunken fishingboats standing out of the gray chop. Nothing moving out there. Anything that could move had long been blown away. His leg was throbbing and he pulled away the dressing and disinfected the wound and looked at it. The flesh swollen and discolored in the truss of the black stitching. He dressed it and pulled his bloodstiffened trousers on.

They spent the day there, sitting among the boxes and crates. You have to talk to me, he said.

I'm talking.

Are you sure?

I'm talking now.

Do you want me to tell you a story?

No.

Why not?

The boy looked at him and looked away.

Why not?

Those stories are not true.

They dont have to be true. They're stories.

Yes. But in the stories we're always helping people and we dont help people.

Why dont you tell me a story?

I dont want to.

Okay.

I dont have any stories to tell.

You could tell me a story about yourself.

You already know all the stories about me. You were there.

You have stories inside that I dont know about.

You mean like dreams?

Like dreams. Or just things that you think about.

Yeah, but stories are supposed to be happy.

They dont have to be.

You always tell happy stories.

You dont have any happy ones?

They're more like real life.

But my stories are not.

Your stories are not. No.

The man watched him. Real life is pretty bad?

What do you think?

Well, I think we're still here. A lot of bad things have happened but we're still here.

Yeah.

You dont think that's so great.

It's okay.

They'd pulled a worktable up to the windows and spread out their blankets and the boy was lying there on his stomach looking out across the bay. The man sat with his leg stretched out. On the blanket between them were the two pistols and the box of flares. After a while the man said: I think it's pretty good. It's a pretty good story. It counts for something.

It's okay, Papa. I just want to have a little quiet time.

What about dreams? You used to tell me dreams sometimes.

I dont want to talk about anything.

Okay.

I dont have good dreams anyway. They're always about something bad happening. You said that was okay because good dreams are not a good sign.

Maybe. I dont know.

When you wake up coughing you walk out along the road or somewhere but I can still hear you coughing.

I'm sorry.

One time I heard you crying.

I know.

So if I shouldnt cry you shouldnt cry either.

Okay.

Is your leg going to get better?

Yes.

You're not just saying that.

No.

Because it looks really hurt.

It's not that bad.

The man was trying to kill us. Wasnt he.

Yes. He was.

Did you kill him?

No.

Is that the truth?

Yes.

Okay.

Is that all right?

Yes.

I thought you didnt want to talk?

I dont.

They left two days later, the man limping along behind the cart and the boy keeping close to his side until they cleared the outskirts of the town. The road ran along the flat gray coast and there were drifts of sand in the road that the winds had left there. It made for heavy going and they had to shovel their way in places with a plank they carried in the lower rack of the cart. They walked out down the beach and sat in the lee of the dunes and studied the map. They'd brought the burner with them and they heated water and made tea and sat wrapped in their blankets against the wind. Downshore the weathered timbers of an ancient ship. Gray and sandscrubbed beams, old handturned scarpbolts. The pitted iron hardware deep lilac in color, smeltered in some bloomery in Cadiz or Bristol and beaten out on a blackened anvil, good to last three hundred years against the sea. The following day they passed through the boarded ruins of a seaside resort and took the road inland through a pine wood, the long straight blacktop drifted in pineneedles, the wind in the dark trees.

He sat in the road at noon in the best light there would be and snipped the sutures with the scissors and put the scissors back in the kit and took out the clamp. Then he set about pulling the small black threads from his skin, pressing down with the flat of his thumb. The boy sat in the road watching. The man fastened the clamp over the ends of the threads and pulled them out one by one. Small pinlets of blood. When he was done he put away the clamp and taped gauze over the wound and then stood and pulled his trousers up and handed the kit to the boy to put away.

That hurt, didnt it? the boy said.

Yes. It did.

Are you real brave?

Just medium.

What's the bravest thing you ever did?

He spat into the road a bloody phlegm. Getting up this morning, he said.

Really?

No. Dont listen to me. Come on, let's go.

In the evening the murky shape of another coastal city, the cluster of tall buildings vaguely askew. He thought the iron armatures had softened in the heat and then reset again to leave the buildings standing out of true. The melted window glass hung frozen down the walls like icing on a cake. They went on. In the nights sometimes now he'd wake in the black and freezing waste out of softly colored worlds of human love, the songs of birds, the sun.

He leaned his forehead on his arms crossed upon the bar handle of the cart and coughed. He spat a bloody drool. More and more he had to stop and rest. The boy watched him. In some other world the child would already have begun to vacate him from his life. But he had no life other. He knew the boy lay awake in the night and listened to hear if he were breathing.

The days sloughed past uncounted and uncalendared. Along the interstate in the distance long lines of charred and rusting cars. The raw rims of the wheels sitting in a stiff gray sludge of melted rubber, in blackened rings of wire. The incinerate corpses shrunk to the size of a child and propped on the bare springs of the seats. Ten thousand dreams ensepulchred within their crozzled hearts. They went on. Treading the dead world under like rats on a wheel. The nights dead still and deader black. So cold. They talked hardly at all. He coughed all the time and the boy watched him spitting blood. Slumping along. Filthy, ragged, hopeless. He'd stop and lean on the cart and the boy would go on and then stop and look back and he would raise his weeping eyes and see him standing there in the road looking back at him from some unimaginable future, glowing in that waste like a tabernacle.

The road crossed a dried slough where pipes of ice stood out of the frozen mud like formations in a cave. The remains of an old fire by the side of the road. Beyond that a long concrete causeway. A dead swamp. Dead trees standing out of the gray water trailing gray and relic hagmoss. The silky spills of ash against the curbing. He stood leaning on the gritty concrete rail. Perhaps in the world's destruction it would be possible at last to see how it was made. Oceans, mountains. The ponderous counterspectacle of things ceasing to be. The sweeping waste, hydroptic and coldly secular. The silence.

They'd begun to come upon dead windfalls of pine-trees, great swaths of ruin cut through the countryside. The wreckage of buildings strewn over the landscape and skeins of wire from the roadside poles garbled like knitting. The road was littered with debris and it was work to get the cart through. Finally they just sat by the side of the road and stared at what was before them. Roofs of houses, the trunks of trees. A boat. The open sky beyond where in the distance the sullen sea lagged and shifted.

They sorted through the wreckage strewn along the road and in the end he came up with a canvas bag that he could tote over his shoulder and a small suitcase for the boy. They packed their blankets and the tarp and what was left of the canned goods and set out again with their knapsacks and their bags leaving the cart behind. Clambering through the ruins. Slow going. He had to stop and rest. He sat in a roadside sofa, the cushions bloated in the damp. Bent over, coughing. He pulled the bloodstained mask from his face and got up and rinsed it in the ditch and wrung it out and then just stood there in the road. His breath pluming white. Winter was already upon them. He turned and looked at the boy. Standing with his suitcase like an orphan waiting for a bus.

In two days' time they came to a broad tidal river where the bridge lay collapsed in the slow moving water. They sat on the broken abutment of the road and watched the river backing upon itself and coiling over the iron trellis-work. He looked across the water to the country beyond.

What are we going to do Papa? he said.

Well what are we, said the boy.

They walked out the long spit of tidal mud where a small boat lay half buried and stood there looking at it. It was altogether derelict. There was rain in the wind. They trudged up the beach with their baggage looking for shelter but they found none. He scuffled together a pile of the bonecolored wood that lay along the shore and got a fire going and they sat in the dunes with the tarp over them and watched the cold rain coming in from the north. It fell harder, dimpling the sand. The fire steamed and the smoke swung in slow coils and the boy curled up under the pattering tarp and soon he was asleep. The man pulled the plastic over himself in a hood and watched the gray sea shrouded away out there in the rain and watched the surf break along the shore and draw away again over the dark and stippled sand.

The next day they headed inland. A vast low swale where ferns and hydrangeas and wild orchids lived on in ashen effigies which the wind had not yet reached. Their progress was a torture. In two days when they came out upon a road he set the bag down and sat bent over with his arms crossed at his chest and coughed till he could cough no more. Two more days and they may have traveled ten miles. They crossed the river and a short ways on they came to a crossroads. Downcountry a storm had passed over the isthmus and leveled the dead black trees from east to west like weeds in the floor of a stream. Here they camped and when he lay down he knew that he could go no further and that this was the place where he would die. The boy sat watching him, his eyes welling. Oh Papa, he said.

He watched him come through the grass and kneel with the cup of water he'd fetched. There was light all about him. He took the cup and drank and lay back. They had for food a single tin of peaches but he made the boy eat it and he would not take any. I cant, he said. It's all right.

I'll save your half.

Okay. You save it until tomorrow.

He took the cup and moved away and when he moved the light moved with him. He'd wanted to try and make a tent out of the tarp but the man would not let him. He said that he didnt want anything covering him. He lay watching the boy at the fire. He wanted to be able to see. Look around you, he said. There is no prophet in the earth's long chronicle who's not honored here today. Whatever form you spoke of you were right.

The boy thought he smelled wet ash on the wind. He went up the road and come dragging back a piece of plywood from the roadside trash and he drove sticks into the ground with a rock and made of the plywood a rickety leanto but in the end it didnt rain. He left the flarepistol and took the revolver with him and he scoured the countryside for anything to eat but he came back emptyhanded. The man took his hand, wheezing. You need to go on, he said. I cant go with you. You need to keep going. You dont know what might be down the road. We were always lucky. You'll be lucky again. You'll see. Just go. It's all right.

I cant.

It's all right. This has been a long time coming. Now it's here. Keep going south. Do everything the way we did it.

You're going to be okay, Papa. You have to.

No I'm not. Keep the gun with you at all times. You

need to find the good guys but you cant take any chances. No chances. Do you hear?

I want to be with you.

You cant.

Please.

You cant. You have to carry the fire.

I dont know how to.

Yes you do.

Is it real? The fire?

Yes it is.

Where is it? I dont know where it is.

Yes you do. It's inside you. It was always there. I can see it.

Just take me with you. Please.

I cant.

Please, Papa.

I cant. I cant hold my son dead in my arms. I thought I could but I cant.

You said you wouldnt ever leave me.

I know. I'm sorry. You have my whole heart. You always did. You're the best guy. You always were. If I'm not here you can still talk to me. You can talk to me and I'll talk to you. You'll see.

Will I hear you?

Yes. You will. You have to make it like talk that you imagine. And you'll hear me. You have to practice. Just dont give up. Okay?

Okay.

Okay.

I'm really scared Papa.

I know. But you'll be okay. You're going to be lucky. I know you are. I've got to stop talking. I'm going to start coughing again.

It's okay, Papa. You dont have to talk. It's okay.

He went down the road as far as he dared and then he came back. His father was asleep. He sat with him under the plywood and watched him. He closed his eyes and talked to him and he kept his eyes closed and listened. Then he tried again.

He woke in the darkness, coughing softly. He lay listening. The boy sat by the fire wrapped in a blanket watching him. Drip of water. A fading light. Old dreams encroached upon the waking world. The dripping was in the cave. The light was a candle which the boy bore in a ringstick of beaten copper. The wax spattered on the stones. Tracks of unknown creatures in the mortified loess. In that cold corridor they had reached the point of no return which was measured from the first solely by the light they carried with them.

Do you remember that little boy, Papa?

Yes. I remember him.

Do you think that he's all right that little boy?

Oh yes. I think he's all right.

Do you think he was lost?

No. I dont think he was lost.

I'm scared that he was lost.

I think he's all right.

But who will find him if he's lost? Who will find the little boy?

Goodness will find the little boy. It always has. It will again.

He slept close to his father that night and held him but when he woke in the morning his father was cold and stiff. He sat there a long time weeping and then he got up and walked out through the woods to the road. When he came back he knelt beside his father and held his cold hand and said his name over and over again.

He stayed three days and then he walked out to the road and he looked down the road and he looked back the way they had come. Someone was coming. He started to turn and go back into the woods but he didnt. He just stood in the road and waited, the pistol in his hand. He'd piled all the blankets on his father and he was cold and he was hungry. The man that hove into view and stood there looking at him was dressed in a gray and yellow ski parka. He carried a shotgun upside down over his shoulder on a braided leather lanyard and he wore a nylon bandolier filled with shells for the gun. A veteran of old skirmishes, bearded, scarred across his cheek and the bone stoven and the one eye wandering. When he spoke his mouth worked imperfectly, and when he smiled.

Where's the man you were with?

He died.

Was that your father?

Yes. He was my papa.

I'm sorry.

I dont know what to do.

I think you should come with me.

Are you one of the good guys?

The man pulled back the hood from his face. His hair was long and matted. He looked at the sky. As if there were anything there to be seen. He looked at the boy. Yeah, he said. I'm one of the good guys. Why dont you put the pistol away?

I'm not supposed to let anyone take the pistol. No matter what.

I dont want your pistol. I just dont want you pointing it at me.

Okay.

Where's your stuff?

We dont have much stuff.

Have you got a sleeping bag?

No.

What have you got? Some blankets?

My papa's wrapped in them.

Show me.

The boy didnt move. The man watched him. He squatted on one knee and swung the shotgun up from under his arm and stood it in the road and leaned on the forestock. The shotgun shells in the loops of the bandolier were handloaded and the ends sealed with candlewax. He smelled of woodsmoke. Look, he said. You got two choices here. There was some discussion about whether to even come after you at all. You can stay here with your papa and die or you can go with me. If you stay you need to keep out of the road. I dont know how you made it this far. But you should go with me. You'll be all right.

How do I know you're one of the good guys?

You dont. You'll have to take a shot.

Are you carrying the fire?

Am I what?

Carrying the fire.

You're kind of weirded out, arent you?

No.

Just a little.

Yeah.

That's okay.

So are you?

What, carrying the fire?

Yes.

Yeah. We are.

Do you have any kids?

We do.

Do you have a little boy?

We have a little boy and we have a little girl.

How old is he?

He's about your age. Maybe a little older.

And you didnt eat them.

No.

You dont eat people.

No. We dont eat people.

And I can go with you?

Yes. You can.

Okay then.

Okay.

They went into the woods and the man squatted and looked at the gray and wasted figure under the tilted sheet of plywood. Are these all the blankets you have?

Yes.

Is that your suitcase?

Yes.

He stood. He looked at the boy. Why dont you go back out to the road and wait for me. I'll bring the blankets and everything.

What about my papa?

What about him.

We cant just leave him here.

Yes we can.

I dont want people to see him.

There's no one to see him.

Can I cover him with leaves?

The wind will blow them away.

Could we cover him with one of the blankets?

Yes. I'll do it. Go on now.

Okay.

He waited in the road and when the man came out of the woods he was carrying the suitcase and he had the blankets over his shoulder. He sorted through them and handed one to the boy. Here, he said. Wrap this around you. You're cold. The boy tried to hand him the pistol but he wouldnt take it. You hold onto that, he said.

Okay.

Do you know how to shoot it?

Yes.

Okay.

What about my papa?

There's nothing else to be done.

I think I want to say goodbye to him.

Will you be all right?

Yes.

Go ahead. I'll wait for you.

He walked back into the woods and knelt beside his father. He was wrapped in a blanket as the man had promised and the boy didnt uncover him but he sat beside him and he was crying and he couldnt stop. He cried for a long time. I'll talk to you every day, he whispered. And I wont forget. No matter what. Then he rose and turned and walked back out to the road.

The woman when she saw him put her arms around him and held him. Oh, she said, I am so glad to see you. She would talk to him sometimes about God. He tried to talk to God but the best thing was to talk to his father and he did talk to him and he didnt forget. The woman said that was all right. She said that the breath of God was his breath yet though it pass from man to man through all of time.

Once there were brook trout in the streams in the mountains. You could see them standing in the amber current where the white edges of their fins wimpled softly in the flow. They smelled of moss in your hand. Polished and muscular and torsional. On their backs were vermiculate patterns that were maps of the world in its becoming. Maps and mazes. Of a thing which could not be put back. Not be made right again. In the deep glens where they lived all things were older than man and they hummed of mystery.

picador.com

blog
videos
interviews
extracts